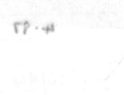

٤٢٠-٨

The Coded Letter
&
Dear Monster

JAVIER TOMEO

THE CODED LETTER
and
DEAR MONSTER

translated from the Spanish by Anthony Edkins

CARCANET

First published in 1991 by
Carcanet Press Limited
208-212 Corn Exchange Buildings
Manchester M4 3BQ

El castillo de la carta cifrada copyright © 1979
Editorial Anagrama, Barcelona; *Amado monstruo* copyright © 1985
Editorial Anagrama, Barcelona.
Translations copyright © 1991 Anthony Edkins
The right of Javier Tomeo to be identified as the writer
of this work and of Anthony Edkins to be identified as the
translator of this work has been asserted by each of them in
accordance with the Copyright, Designs and Patents Act of 1988.

British Library Cataloguing in Publication Data

Tomeo, Javier
 The coded letter and Dear Monster.
 1. Spanish fiction
 I. Title   II. El Castillo de la carta cifrada
 III. Amado Monstruo.   *English*
 863.64 [F]

 ISBN 0 85635 792 8

The publisher acknowledges financial assistance
from the Arts Council of Great Britain

Set in 11pt Concorde by Bryan Williamson, Darwen
Printed and bound in England by SRP Ltd, Exeter

THE CODED LETTER

'Don't worry, Bautista, and stop trembling,' the Marquis said to me that morning. 'What I'm going to get you to do is easy. I'm not one to ask the impossible. You see this letter. It may look like any other letter to you but for me it's a very important one. You must deliver it personally to the Count. I mean, of course, the Count of X, Don Demetrio López del Costillar. You'll have heard me speak of him half a dozen times at least. His castle's on the other side of the valley. To get there, you've a choice of two routes. One crosses the poplar grove and, when you reach the mill, branches off towards the village. The other's direct, crossing the river by the stone bridge and winding up the hill. The latter's shorter, but I prefer you to choose the former. So you choose the former. But when you get to the village, don't let your old chums detain you. Tell all the gossips who waylay you to go to hell. Proceed resolutely along the High Street and after you've passed the Baroness of O's mansion, take the first turning on the right. You must know the Baroness's palace: an enormous barracks of a place in stone, with colossal eaves. I sent you there barely a month ago to find out about the health of that very good friend of mine after her last abortion. Right, leave the Baroness's palace behind you and keep straight on until you reach the stone cross consecrating the crossroads. Station yourself at the foot of the cross and face east. Remember that east is where – up to now, at least – the sun rises. Don't look the other way, then. Focus your attention and, directly opposite on the side of one of the hills which close off the valley's eastern flank, you'll be able to locate the Count's castle. It won't be hard, because it's the only one in that area. You'll also be able to identify it by the big green flag which is always flying on top of the Homage Tower. Have a moment's rest, then continue on your way. If you go at a good pace, it won't take more than an hour to reach the perimeter wall. Go through the outer gateway and proceed along the drive, which zig-zags across the garden. You'll get to the main gate in a couple of minutes. An impressive gate, I warn you. I remember it as equipped with bolts and powerful hinges. In my day, it gave every visitor a vague feeling of horror. Overcome your fears, and resort to the knocker. Knock resolutely, but not insolently, and it won't be long before they answer. I don't know whether the Count will have changed his steward after all this time. Four lustra ago you could have reckoned on coming across the most sinister servant in the whole region. A fellow with an insolent tongue and a stealthy walk, who spoke in a whisper. That man must have been about sixty, so if he were still alive, he'd be over eighty today. Too old for active service. Anyway, whosoever the servant be, the fact is they've let you in. You're already beneath the hall's Gothic vault. Clearly enunciate the Count's name, and wait. Another servant arrives and begins to lead you – along dark and intricate passage-ways – to Don Demetrio's study. It'll be a long way, I can tell you that in advance. You'll pass through draw-ing-rooms, go down some staircases, go up others, turn towards the right, then towards the left and, after half an hour's march you'll enter a small living-room, lit by a pair of oil-lamps, whose walls are decorated with beautiful Chinese panelling. You'll leave through another door hidden behind a curtain, advance down more passageways, make further left and right turns, and you'll then begin to understand that it's never easy to reach the person we seek. The hearts of all those we need are always at the centre of a labyrinth. However, during the journey you'll see some wonderful objects. Heraldic trophies, sombre tapestries, magic sculptures, extremely beautiful paintings. At last the servant pushes open an enormous mahogany door and invites you to enter. You'll now find yourself in an immense drawing-room, with a very high ceiling. The sun's feeble rays are penetrating the long, narrow, multi-coloured stained-glass windows. The Count is lying on a couch. He raises an arm and flutters his fingers, asking you to approach. You obey, you hand him the letter and you request that he reads it in your presence. Formulate the desire with due humility, giving him to understand that I am particularly concerned that things be done in this way. Having made this petition – which, surely, will not occasion objections – hold your breath and wait. Show yourself to be patient. I gather the Count doesn't see very well any more. It's therefore likely that it'll take him more than two hours to read the two manuscript sheets I'm sending him. What's more, he's a suspicious man and he'll re-read the letter three or four times, trying to find in the text some hidden affront, some secret calumny. While he's reading and re-reading the missive, restrict yourself to waiting steadfastly beside the couch, your eyes on the floor. Your attitude should be, not merely respectful, but decidedly submissive. Don't show any interest in the room's decoration. I'm telling you this, so that you're not taken by surprise, suddenly finding yourself in a room crammed with the most extravagant furniture, its walls covered with beautiful hangings and a clock of prodigious dimensions, from which, at the most inopportune moment, the summons to judgement-day can peal. All this, of course, assumes that the Count hasn't decided to change the décor of his sanctum. Anyway – and in spite of your apparent abstraction – you must stay on guard all the time. Don't drop your guard for a moment. You should know that Don Demetrio is a man fond of disconcerting people with the most unexpected questions. Perhaps, barely having started to read the letter – but seeming already interested in its text – he'll raise his eyes from the pages and want to know what you think of, for example, the parcelling of agrarian estates. In similar circumstances, years ago, he used to ask that sort of question. Should you find yourself in this situation, you must evidence your opposition to any bill proposing it. In other words, you must react as if you, too, were a big landowner and the lands to be parcelled were yours. Bear in mind that if the Count detects that you don't support *latifundia* wholeheartedly, he'll tear the letter up into small pieces and send you packing. It'd be a logical reaction, in a way. His reasoning would be more or less the following: What could it matter to me what I'm written by a gentleman whose servant – apart from being lame – doesn't seem properly aware of a matter which so closely concerns us landowners? So be careful, Bautista. Never forget that the Count is a man of strange reactions. And strange tastes. I can tell you, for example, that in his youth he was exclusively – note, I say exclusively – interested in women with a large ovarian capacity. Powerful matrons, capable of undoing a well-built man with a single blow. None of his drinking companions ever saw him look at a woman who weighed less than twelve stone. All his mistresses slept in reinforced beds. Yes, even today I still wonder about that curious obsession of his! Can you tell me, Bautista, what delicate tenderness, what crazy longings for cosmic love-

affairs could justify such a weakness in man who, at that
time, could have weighed little more than eighty-five
pounds? What's more, Don Demetrio had a lot of other
manias. For example, his obsession with uneven numbers. Or his fondness for green, any shade of green.
"There's no colour more restful to the eye," he used to
breathe, contemplating a lettuce. Oh I know very well
that green is the colour of youth, and the Count was not
yet thirty at the time. But I don't believe his dispropor-
tionate liking for that colour was a question of age. As
you know, there are tastes which don't quit us before
the grave. I'm sure Don Demetrio keeps his chromatic
preferences intact. Otherwise, why that emerald green
flag flying day and night from his castle's highest tower?
So much so, Bautista, that you must dress in green to
deliver the letter. Green breeches and a green jerkin.
Green stockings and green shoes. We don't lose anything
doing that. I'll even go so far as to say that if you appear
in any other colour he might refuse to read the letter. A
wrong colour can upset all our predictions. You'll be
wondering: why does the Count prefer green, and not
red, blue or yellow? Who knows, my friend. Remember
there's no discussing colours or tastes. Or at least that's
what the scholastics counselled. I've limited myself to
stating a fact and to suggesting what best you can do. In
fact, I'm restricting myself to describing the main outlines
of your behaviour on a mission which, for me, has the
greatest importance. Moreover, I practise what I preach.
You see this letter's envelope and paper. They're green,
too. I had to investigate half-a-dozen suppliers to find
them. Why *my* present satisfaction at being able to send
a letter written on green paper to a man who appears to
find in that colour the chief source of *his* satisfaction?
I'm going to repeat myself, Bautista: there is no disputing
about tastes. Nobody dared criticize Nero for liking to

watch the fiercest gladiatorial contests through an emerald. That emperor, I'm sure, was hiding something more than mere myopia behind his habit. The need for a nicer world before his eyes, perhaps, without the obligation of admitting such a weakness or giving up bloodshed. Go then, Bautista, to the Count's castle dressed in green. Let's think no more about it. And carry a couple of frogs in your pocket. Green frogs, of course. Picture the scene. The Count has received you without much enthusiasm. He starts to read the letter and is having some difficulties – I'll talk to you about them later. Moreover, his eyesight is weaker than reported. He's irritated. He breaks off, looks up from the letter and unexpectedly is confronted by the two beautiful frogs that you, with foresight, have let loose a moment before. He suddenly feels encouraged. You then explain to him that you brought the frogs at my behest, a detail that ends up predisposing him in our favour. "Let's see, let's see what it is your kind master is telling me," he sighs, starting to read again. Catch a couple of frogs, Bautista. What I'm saying now is no longer a mere suggestion, it's an order. You'll find as many as you like in the pond. Choose the nicest. Neither the smallest nor the biggest. Ones that croak daintily. Keep them in your pocket while the Count, absorbed in reading, is holding the pages a couple of inches from his nose, and release them when he seems on the point of stopping. You ask me why I say "on the point of stopping"? I've reasons for so assuming, Bautista. Many reasons. For one, my writing's bad, as you know. Writing has always tired me. I lack the necessary application to finish forming even the simplest letters. Holding the penholder is a task beyond my strength. So, if I don't want to write gibberish, I have to put myself in the right frame of mind before facing a blank sheet of paper. But with this epistle, Bautista, I set out to be even more complicated. Deliberately, deceitfully, I've written particularly badly. Why? Very simple: when I started to write it, I said to myself that I'd no cause to give the Count the satisfaction of being able to read me without some special effort. That, at least, was the main reason for making my handwriting even more indecipherable. I can tell you, for example, that all the m's in this letter have, instead of three strokes, four. While, for their part, the n's have three, instead of the usual two. Furthermore, the dot on the *i* is always placed over the letter immediately in front of – or behind – the one to which it corresponds. And, as though that were not enough, I don't leave the slightest space between words. Truly, my letter is a single, immense word signifying nothing. Isn't that clever of me, my friend? Come, come, say something! Do you think the Count, with all the will in the world, will be able to read the letter at the first attempt? No, of course not. He'll need at least a couple of hours to read a single sheet. It's even possible that he'll start to lose patience before finishing. And what'll happen if he starts losing his patience? You'd be running some risk, Bautista, I won't try to hide it. When all's said and done, it's you who are delivering the letter, and Don Demetrio is an irascible man. Perhaps, exasperated, he'll flick his seven-stranded whip across your face. Or maybe he'll prefer to hand you over to his lackeys – strapping fellows – to deal with you as they like and they'll give you a beating. Either of these alternatives is bad. So you see how important it is to let the frogs loose at the opportune moment. Not before, not after, but at exactly the right moment. Precisely when you see the Count's face beginning to go red, flushing with anger. So that this poor man, just when he's about to explode, suddenly notices them hopping gracefully on the carpet, green on green. It may be that he'll then forget his displeasure and

end up reconciling himself to the entire world's hieroglyphics. Because, Bautista, you should know that frogs
– above all, green frogs – are animals with a long and
incredible tradition. Sometimes, they go to meet the hero
and entrust him with wonderful secrets, which are worth
an empire. And what if Don Demetrio were to think that
these frogs had a secret for him also, one capable of
giving him back his lost youth? What wouldn't an old
man give to recover his youth? How could we get angry
about having received an incomprehensible letter,
knowing that, in the twinkling of an eye, we were to
become what we had been? However, there's one circumstance in which, on no account, must you let them
loose. You, who want to know everything, will ask: what
circumstance? Very simple, my dear Bautista: in the
event that the Count has received you in company with
his wife, Doña Beatriz, you must not release the frogs.
Or if Doña Beatriz comes into the room while Don
Demetrio is trying to read the letter. Summing up: you
must not free the frogs in the Countess's presence,
because that distinguished lady can't stand frogs. She
couldn't stand them as a child, and I don't believe she'll
have changed. Why? Some strange Freudian complex,
if you must know. What's certain is that if this woman
suddenly noticed them at your feet, she'd be scared to
death. And despite everything, the Count loves his massive wife too deeply to allow someone to frighten her
with impunity. Be careful, then, and if Don Demetrio
receives you in the company of his wife, keep our little
animals in your pocket. Don't free them, even if you see
his knuckles whiten or if he starts cursing my handwriting, or even if the batrachia, irked by their incarceration,
begin to bite you, no matter where. I'm giving you this
advice because it's always better to put up with ordinary
physical violence than with metaphysical rage; it may

even affect your soul's salvation. If, then, the Count –
not having been appeased by the frogs – decides to vent
his anger on your poor body, don't try to defend yourself.
Receive his blows humbly, without a cry. Let that cretin
– because when all's said and done, the Count is no more
than a cretin – know the extent of my servants' fortitude.
Even more: you should respond to the lashes or punches
with a slight smile, a faintly ingratiating smile. I'm not
of course thinking of that arrogant sneer with which, on
mounting the scaffold, some condemned to death insult
their executioner. Nor am I referring to the lewd grimace
of those who find the sublimest pleasure in pain. On the
contrary, your smile must ooze spirituality. In a way, it
ought to lie somewhere between happiness and confidence. While the whip cracks, let your face shine with
the expression of those who put all their hopes of justice
in the next world. I'll say even more – and do forgive me
for belabouring this point – the ideal would be, if it comes
to a beating, for you to go down on your knees before
the Count and meekly offer him your back. Remember
that, ultimately, what's at stake is my own reputation.
You must, therefore, represent me with all possible dignity. I know it's sad always having to climb up and down
someone else's stairway, but that's how things are. Servants, as someone said, should be faithful, misshapen
and fierce. Well, you're already misshapen and fierce –
fierce with your inferiors and equals – so now's your
chance to be faithful as well. What's the matter, Bautista?
Are you trembling? Are you afraid? Are you going to let
the risk of getting a few lashes – decidedly a rather remote
possibility – rob you of the pleasure of knowing that you
are doing me an inestimable service? No, my poor friend!
Don't be frightened in advance! To suffer ahead of time
is to suffer twice! It could also happen that the Count
might react less violently. Who knows? Perhaps he'll

keep the whip for another occasion and try only to pump you for information about the letter's content. Perhaps he'll think I'm simple enough to commit the indiscretion of confiding my secrets and intimate correspondence to servants. If he asks any question of this sort, you must immediately make it quite clear that your ignorance is total. Deny all knowledge as many times as necessary and be quite firm about it, until he understands that, in fact, you know nothing. Swear it, if necessary. Roll your eyes. Fall to your knees, making a cross with your arms. Whatever you prefer, Bautista, but get Don Demetrio to believe in your ignorance. But don't then start crowing, because other dangers could follow. It could happen, for example, that the Count, furious about not having made sense of anything, forces you to eat the letter. If you find yourself in this situation, again you mustn't resist. Bear in mind that the letter's written on rice paper so that, within its limits, it's fairly digestible. Don't lose your composure. Take comfort in thinking about that minute paper-devouring insect, the saccharine bristle-tail, with its cylindrical body and silvery scales. After all, Bautista, you're little more than an insect; I say so without any wish to offend. So be strong – not in rebelling against your fate, but in resigning yourself to your position – and accept with fortitude whatever falls to your lot. Chew the pages with your mouth shut, without making a fuss, as if you were eating a cake. When swallowing, don't let your Adam's apple wobble unduly. Don't allow any emotion to appear on your face. Imitate those admirable English butlers who show no change of expression in the most compromising situations. "Anything more, my lord?" you can ask him, when not a shred of paper is left in your mouth. If Don Demetrio answers negatively, you must bow, letting your body make a forty-five degree angle, and silently retire. If, on the other hand, he commands you to stay where you are, you must remain motionless. Maintain the position you took up when the Count, without any idea of what he was letting himself in for, tore open the envelope and began to read the letter. Don't take any initiative. Let it be he who decides when you should leave. Turn yourself into a pillar of salt. Endure one, two, three hours, whatever is necessary. In your imagination, embark on the most extraordinary journeys – no one can stop you exercising that right – but don't move a finger. If you consider it appropriate, resort to those strange mental games which are capable of creating very complex universes within us. For example, try to imagine a universe in which, instead of stars, third-degree equations or phosphorescent cubic roots shine. Or try inserting yourself into the fascinating world of insects which can offer man so many very profound lessons. The four sheets of paper you've just eaten are still weighing on the stomach. Why not imagine, then, that you've become an abnormally developed saccharine bristletail and try to locate yourself in a gloomy world, barely lit by the distant radiance of venerable parchments? Why not, mounted on your imagination, advance down damp narrow passages, lured by the eloquent perfume of some incunabulum? Imagination's an eternal Spring, Bautista. It should matter little to slaves that, beyond their reach, their masters establish frigid winters. My friend, I can assure you that those who are forced to stand still have many resources at their disposition. Three hours, four hours, five hours. Endure whatever may be necessary. Don't give the Count the pleasure of seeing you faint. Don't worry about me, I shan't punish you, even if you get back at five in the morning. No, you can spend the whole night at Don Demetrio's castle and get back late tomorrow morning. It's almost certain I shan't need you before then. While you're out, I'll read. My insect books await me. Remember that only yesterday you yourself added twelve new volumes to the library. If necessary, I can arrange them on my own. I'm not so useless as some think. While you're motionless in front of the Count, imagining you're a saccharine bristletail, I can believe that I've been changed into another lowly insect, open to death at any moment from some hiker's boot. I'll be very frank with you, Bautista; I've often felt envious of those minute creatures who are born and who live and die unaware of the passage of time. Oh yes! How happy I'd be if I were able to change myself into, for example, one of those mantis in love with their own beauty! Probably my favourite insect, Bautista. Do you know it? In this world there's nothing more beautiful. The lower part of its body resembles a branch of dead leaves from which, at the end of a long narrow tail, protrudes the miracle of a pink, violet, blue and purple petal. Even its forelegs – the ones that grasp its prey – have a long membranous protraction which could easily pass for an orchid. Can you imagine such beauty? All right, I'm not going to argue. Not everything's cut and dried. Even insects have their misgivings and doubts. One day or another, the beautiful mantis looking at itself in the pond's mirror, will have felt confused, trying to discern its true nature. Perhaps it asked itself: Who am I? What if I were not that cruel insect I think myself to be? What if I were really a flower? What I'm trying to tell you, Bautista, is that maybe even insects have their problems. Even problems of loneliness. Think of glow-worms, for example. They're prosaic and insignificant during the day. When night comes, however, they become fantastic torchbearers, and their cold greenish light can be constant or intermittent, according to sex, species and environmental conditions. Don't you find that fascinating? Now try to imagine the scene. The male glow-worm feels lonely. He flashes his amorous message and two seconds later the female responds. Like a clock. She too needs company. She doesn't care whether the reply comes now or comes later; what she really wants is to be needed. Who, then, could dare say that glow-worms don't have problems of loneliness? If they didn't, would they take the trouble to exchange so many illuminated messages? The sad thing is, Bautista, that these insects' amorous spark may be the sure cause of their ruin. Love is always stalked by cold-blooded monsters. There, for example, is the glow-worm's enemy, the frog. He devours hundreds of them and, later, on hot summer nights, you can see him shining at the edge of the pool. His victims' light and beauty live on in the cretin's belly. Have you noticed? Well, the following question comes to mind: supposing I'd once been able to be a glow-worm, where could I find my lost beauty today? In what belly does the light, which once distinguished me from all other men, repose? But I'm getting away from the only thing that interests us. I've a terrible tendency to digress. Let's get back to our business. I told you earlier, you must remain absolutely still all the time you're with Don Demetrio. I want him to envy me for having such a patient, silent servant. So, prudence above all, be very prudent. Control your nerves. But be ready at all times to deal with emergencies. An example: imagine that, at the most unexpected moment, the frogs begin to croak. What should you do then? I can't exactly say, Bautista, but I'm going to tell you what you mustn't do: on no account smile, however amusing the situation may seem to you. Let the frogs croak as much as they like but, for the love of God, don't smile. I say this for your own good. A smile from you in such circumstances could be highly dangerous. It could mean a sort of declaration of war. It could amount to an unacceptable insolence, particularly just after having received a blow or having been forced to swallow four sheets of paper. Don't you know, Bautista, that nothing annoys winners more than the discovery that the losers' morale remains intact? I'm telling you quite clearly: if the frogs begin to croak and you, without being able to help it, burst into laughter, the Count's reaction could be genuinely dangerous. He might be capable of tying you to the rack, which he must still have in the castle cellars, or of putting you under the scythe which swings from the torture chamber's ceiling like a pendulum. Don Demetrio's a cretin – as I've already told you – but, when all's said and done, he's a gentleman of ancient lineage and in no way could he tolerate the challenge of a peasant. Once you've freed them, let the frogs strike out on their own. Let 'em croak till they burst, but don't you smile. Never change your position. Be like a suit of armour. Courage! Are you starting to tremble again? Does it all seem to you terribly complicated? Are you frightened that your strength will fail? I think I can read your thoughts. You'd like to know the letter's content, in case the Count furiously seizes you by the throat and commands you to read it. I'm bound to admit that your wish seems quite reasonable to me, because the worst thing that can happen to a man is to die without being able to provide a fitting answer. But how can I explain my letter to you, if I myself don't really know what I've written? Let's see, let me think, allow me to recall some item…Ah memory, cruel enemy of my happiness! What have I written to the Count? We'll see…I think I recall that, in the opening paragraphs, I loosely enlarge on the dangers that stimulants such as tobacco, alcohol and coffee entail for the human organism. I also refer to the risks which heavy meals afford. An unusual opening for any letter, I realize, but nothing else occurred to me.

What's odd is that, in this case, these recommendations are utterly inappropriate. Quite a few people who know Don Demetrio well would ask me why I waste my time giving this kind of advice to a man who, apart from his liking for fat women, was famous throughout the district for his sobriety and good habits. Because the Count didn't smoke or drink and hardly permitted himself the luxury of eating any more than was necessary to keep going. Mind you, he never missed a banquet, but he insulted all of us with his hateful frugality. A truly surprising attitude which, later, I began to find somewhat suspicious. Finally, I came to the conclusion that the man couldn't be as frugal as he tried to make us believe. I asked myself the following question: Who has seen Don Demetrio eating in his private chambers, alone except for his Persian cat? There's a saying – and forgive me, Bautista, for resorting to such a commonplace form of wisdom – that throws quite a lot of light on the matter: There's little difference between a feast and a bellyful. My conclusion: I now suspect that the Count turns up at public banquets with a full belly. I'll accept that he doesn't smoke or drink, but I find it much harder to believe a man can get through the day on a few olives, a hard-boiled egg and a tiny drop of mineral water. Especially knowing that Don Demetrio comes from a family of gluttons. I didn't think of that until quite recently, when I suddenly remembered that, for a bet, Don Demetrio's parents ate between them a small calf, four chickens and thirty bananas. Bearing in mind this family background, I ask myself: Can a son so easily give up his parents' gastronomic habits? Don't we perhaps inherit stomach from our parents – or, at least, a stomachic structure – in the same way as we inherit blood and lineage? You see, Bautista, that my suggestions may not be so inappropriate after all. I'm almost

certain now that Don Demetrio has always hidden secret
vices behind his façade of sobriety. This rogue must be
much more a friend of the table than he's tried to have
us believe. But I don't want you to think that I'm always
out to grind my own axe. Let's assume that the Count is
really a man without appetite, that all his meals can be
narrowed down to that dozen or so olives and that famous hard-boiled egg. All right, that's his funeral! Anyway,
you needn't worry about my recommendations, Bautista.
Do you know why? It's simple: because he won't be able
to decipher them. Here you have one of the great advantages bestowed by bad handwriting: our addressees need
never annoy us. If we advise something and they don't
follow our advice, we can always console ourselves by
thinking, if they don't act on it, it's because they don't
understand. Thus, half an hour after having begun to
read the letter, Don Demetrio still won't know whether
I'm counselling moderation at table or if I'm talking to
him about panspermatogenesis, that theory which seeks
to explain the appearance of life through the artificial
dissemination of living seeds brought to our world by
ancient meteorites. You look doubtful, Bautista! Have
you already forgotten that all the words in my letter –
absolutely all except for the signature – are joined
together, without any break in continuity? Have you
also forgotten the subtle disguising of m's and n's? And
the dot on the *i*, always coming a little before, or a little
after? There's another trick I've resorted to which I still
haven't told you about: my writing's so small that no one
can read it, not even with a magnifying glass. A veritable
microscopic miniature. Ha, Bautista! Have you ever met
anyone more farsighted? Ships carry two anchors for a
good reason, Bautista: forewarned is forearmed. Be careful, take care. Never go all out, or say all you know, or
judge all you see, or believe all you hear. Once misfortune

comes, it makes us wary and over-cautious, but happiness makes us blind. My letter is a prodigy of obscurity, because obscurity is the very heaven of devout women and houris. I'm very fond of sayings this morning, because I don't want to lose any chance of making you fully understand what my ideas are. In darkness, goes another of those sayings, mystery reigns. But I want to be straight with you. I don't want you to leave this room shrugging your shoulders. Ha! You're surprised, my friend? Your master's perspicacity amazes you? You're looking at me strangely, as if you're beginning to know me at last this morning. But don't let's be too optimistic, and let's continue with our precautions. Let's suppose that, in spite of everything and after arduous effort, the Count manages to decipher a few words here and there. The word coffee, for example, or tobacco. Do you think that possibility worries me? Not a bit. Tell me how it could help, knowing a word on its own. What could it suggest to him, among the thousands that surround it? Many different and even contradictory things can be written about tobacco, for example. How could Don Demetrio know if I'm referring to nicotine poisoning or to the so-called tobacco heart manifested by some smokers? The same considerations apply to coffee. Starting from that simple word, how does one deduce what follows? Many things can also be said about coffee: Ethiopian monks drink it to withstand a whole night of prayer, for example, or this: its use – and even abuse – gave an analytical ability to men who, in classical civilizations, were over-fond of wine. It can also be said, although it's a truism, that coffee is always black because, if it was another colour, it would cease to be coffee. Do you see? A whole universe of interpretations. Each word, however humble, confronts us with a crossroads, and any direction we take can be valid. In short, neither the word "coffee" nor the word "tobacco", on their own, mean a great deal. And one could say almost the same about men, because, individually, man doesn't amount to much either. Let's imagine that someone tries to interpret mankind through me, and writes a massive treatise on Humanity. The book, without doubt, would be a fiasco, because – by luck or misfortune – I am like nobody else. I don't coincide – or I coincide very little – with my fellow-men. Do you believe there are many men who could write letters like this one? You're raising your eyebrows, Bautista. You don't begin to understand me. You can't hide your uneasiness. You're wondering why I'm troubling to send a letter rigged so its recipient can't read it. You're saying: why make life so complicated? Wouldn't it have been easier to save yourself the trouble and to let things go on as they have been? No, Bautista, it wouldn't have been easier. By now, you should know that. I am, in spite of everything, a man who feels the over-riding need to communicate with others. I've been silent too long, and the desire to write letters and to find ideal recipients has been born in me with this new Spring. I realize I'm not alone in this, because many people, condemned to silence and solitude, are better able to bear their lot, thanks to the epistolary genre. Careful: the difficulty arises when we sit in front of a blank sheet of paper, pen at the ready. My God, what anxious moments! How can we dare write perfectly legible letters when the risk exists that the recipient doesn't share our ideas? Worse still: how can we possibly write a letter when we don't know what to say or have nothing to say? What formulas can we resort to when, having squeezed our souls, we find in them not a drop of happiness to offer to others? That's a serious problem, my friend, because, in spite of everything, we're unable to resign ourselves to silence. Given this servitude, doesn't it seem logical to you that I'd try to mask my bitterness by making confusing references to gluttony, coffee and tobacco, and to hope that someone will try to decipher my hieroglyphics at a later date? That, and no other, is the reason for this letter, my dear Bautista. To know that someone will be somehow thinking about me this very evening. Now do you understand me better? Are you still being stubbornly uneasy? Don't let's think about it any more and let's deliver my letter to the Count. But let's do so with the secret hope that he won't understand a single word of what I write. I grant myself the advantage of obscurity. At night all cats are grey. Or as that other man said: all wheat resembles flour. After all, we're at the height of a civilization of cleverly contrived hoax. Look at the majority of today's painters. Entertainers for the consumer society. All they do is complicate and colour their mediocrities. We, too, are complicating our mediocrity and we trust that Don Demetrio won't be able to decipher it. But we shan't celebrate prematurely. You must know that saying which goes: man proposes, God disposes. If wishes were horses, beggars would ride. I trust that Don Demetrio won't understand the letter, but a risk remains that can't be ignored. The Count, in spite of his ancient lineage, is not a very intelligent man. In our schooldays he could barely understand the same reading book that we, his companions, had read as beginners. Later, despite powerful influence, he wasn't able to get into University. I don't imagine he's been able to make up for lost time during these years, because his problem was congenital intellectual limitation, not lack of will-power. So we can't rule out the possibility that, having failed to read the letter, he'll blame, not the hand-writing, but his own stupidity. In which case, I know him well enough to be able to tell you right now that he'll never be reconciled to admitting his ignorance. Don

Demetrio was always extremely proud. As proud as that beetle who, when they were going to shoe the Pasha's horse, had the idea of holding out his own foot. Taking into account this facet of his personality, what'll be his reaction faced with my gibberish? Hold tight, Bautista, because what I'm going to tell you now is quite funny: it's possible that the Count, putting the letter in his pocket, will turn to you condescendingly and say that he willingly accepts my invitation to a pheasant shoot. He'll stake all on one throw, in a bid to end the humiliation of receiving a letter he's incapable of reading. If that really happens, make no comment. Don't think of humiliating him further by smiling suspiciously. Limit yourself to a quick nod of assent. But remember that this business of shooting pheasants is absolutely untrue. Don't let him deceive you. Always remember that I've restricted myself in the letter to the agglutination of a sequence of words without very much meaning. The only thing that mattered to me when I was writing it – and the only thing that goes on mattering – was – and is – that the Count receive it this same evening and that, from the very first moment, he knows that it is precisely I who am sending it. Look where it says "sender". You can read my name quite clearly. Do you see? It's printed, a child could read it. The Count can remain in no doubt about the sender's identity. An old friend, a schoolmate and, later, a companion in the frolics and follies of youth, although, to be frank, Don Demetrio was not especially distinguished by his festive spirit. We were also messmates, in the Archduke's Regiment of Hussars. No small thing, sharing for three long years all the unpleasantness of life in barracks. He'll remember me very well, I'm sure. Could it be that you don't remember your fellow-conscripts, Bautista? Where did you serve? In the Infantry? The Artillery? Did you perhaps serve in the Engineers?

Oh Bautista! I deserve a kick in the rear. You're lame!
I'd forgotten you'd got one leg longer than the other!
They surely classified you completely unfit. It doesn't
matter. Don't pull such a face, you shouldn't be ashamed
of being lame! Would you like me to list right away the
illustrious lame? Take heart, my friend, I can assure you
that not everyone can presume to have a limp as graceful
as yours. Seeing you walk is a delight. So much so that
I often wonder whether you were born for peace and
love exclusively. I say this because I know on good
authority that in this district alone more than a few ladies
would give quite a lot for your services. They envy me,
I know it well. I've had several anonymous approaches
in this respect. Among them, one from a Duchess. You'll
ask: how does the Marquis know it was a Duchess? And
it wouldn't be unreasonable to ask, because anonymous
letters aren't signed, even with a ducal crown. But I know
very well that behind one of those anonymous missives
beats the passionate heart of a Duchess, still good-look-
ing. Even today, after so many years of abstinence, I can
identify a lady's ancestry by the trace of perfume she
leaves in her letters. So you see how things are, Bautista.
I'm sure that, if it weren't for your being lame, none of
these ladies would feel the slightest interest in your
person. But your limp – I'm saying this very frankly, so
that you can put aside all your complexes – is a randy
limp, which endows your rump with a strange circular
movement. You walk, Bautista, and it's as if you were
announcing: Here I am, my ladies, and we only have a
little time to live. And you know, my friend, what the
majority of women are like today. Why should we
deceive ourselves? I'm apart from the world, but I keep
in touch with what's going on out there. They've never
fought for their rights more strongly than now, but, at
the same time, there have never been so many who have

devoted themselves to consumerism with such pleasure and so blatantly. Then there are the others, those on the right, so to speak. There are great numbers of wives who don't lack for excitement. Speaking plainly, Bautista, the flesh of others has never been easier than now. What does it matter whether or not you did military service, in the light of the enormous advantage your limp affords. Never mind about the Infantry or the Artillery, or about being completely unfit. Why should you worry about these little things, when barrack gates are besieged by conscientious objectors? Be lame, my friend, be lame, and don't be ashamed of it, it's better to be gracefully lame than not to be graceful, to have flat feet and stamp around like a bear. Although thinking about it calmly – it just occurs to me – this special limp of yours may land us in some annoying situations. You'll see when I try to explain. We've already mentioned the possibility that Don Demetrio may receive you accompanied by the Countess, and I told you that, if this happens, you must forget about the frogs in your pocket. But now I must add that if you find yourself in the presence of Don Demetrio's wife, don't move: neither set free the frogs nor move a step. Stay still until Doña Beatriz disappears. I'll tell you why. The Count is a jealous man. He always was, and according to my latest information, he goes on being so. You know what jealous people are like. They are more prone to self-love than to love. Jealousy's a self-engendering monster. Don Demetrio is jealous of both light and wind, as the song goes. If you begin to walk, waggling your bottom, and the Countess, who's always on the lookout for an opportunity, can't help her eyes lighting up, all hell could break loose. There's even a possibility that Don Demetrio, without more ado, could kill you. You and, of course, her. Reflect a moment, Bautista, how sad it would be to die for a woman whom we haven't even had in our arms. Act cautiously, be prudent and avoid all movement in Doña Beatriz's presence. Don't move even if the Count insists that you may withdraw. Stoutly resist all such indications and even orders. Don't move, but, through your sacrificial expression, let the Count know that you'd like to move, if you could do so without unleashing a tragedy. You understand me, Bautista? I'd be very unhappy if you were to die at the hand of a jealous husband – blamelessly, to boot. What would I do, with you dead? Where could I find another servant like you? Who, like my good Bautista, would willingly reconcile himself to wearing green and to carrying a couple of frogs in his pockets? Because, regardless of whether or not you're able to use them when the moment arrives, these frogs are still extremely important in my view. As soon as you leave this room, you must go to the pond and capture a couple. As I said earlier, choose the ones with the worst croak. And the ugliest. Of course, all frogs are ugly, but even in ugliness, there are degrees. Once you've caught them, bring them for me to look at. And I'll give you the letter. Dress in green, then off you go without more ado to the Count's castle. Don't be persuaded to deliver the letter to anyone except Don Demetrio himself. While the Count is trying to decipher my letter, let the frogs loose, precisely when he's beginning to get angry. You may have to be crafty. But don't free them, if his wife's there. In either case, stand there attentively, respectfully, silently. If, in spite of having been agreeably surprised by the batrachians' green, the Count is annoyed, even to the point of hitting you, you mustn't dodge the blows. Put up with them, smiling resignedly. Remember that he who laughs last, laughs longest. If he sends you packing, leave the room without saying a word. Unless Doña Beatriz is there, then don't move at all. A frightfully important point, because it concerns your survival. If he makes you eat the letter, do so. And if he tries to pump you about its content, remember you know nothing. Not even what I told you earlier about coffee and tobacco. You know nothing. Don't be deceived if the Count, with a pontifical air, talks about special invitations, pheasants, or anything similar. Don't forget that if he resorts to such tactics, it'll only be to disguise his ignorance. It may also happen that, without going so far as a whip, Don Demetrio will give you a verbal lashing. Perhaps, while tearing up the letter, he'll vent his anger, calling you scoundrel, peasant, wretch, rotter, rogue. Perhaps he'll call you worm, mouthing the word. Don't get angry. Remember that insults ignored, vanish. "All right," – say to him with a slight smile – "it's generous of you to call me a worm. I am, in fact, a worm. I breathe through my skin and my digestive tract runs from one end of my body to the other. I'm not clever, neither am I handsome. I've neither wings nor feet. But, dragging myself along, I can get anywhere." Say all this without being self-important, without pretending to be an entomologist. Adopt the unabashed manner of those comedians who, after getting the worst insults, answer the public back with the same kind of cutting remark, but without departing from an appropriate climate of merriment and fun. Do you follow me, Bautista? If Don Demetrio insults you, keep up your courage. And don't get impatient with all this advice I'm giving you. In this field, I prefer to sin through commission rather than omission. Better to be safe than sorry, I've always thought. Bear in mind, moreover, that you're not really involved in this intrigue. You're merely a messenger with an unintelligible letter. Nothing more than that. You couldn't play another role, even if you wanted to, because it's impossible for you – or for any of your class – to understand our anguish and loneliness. Ducks belong to the same family as swans, but they are – and will always be – ducks. That's how things are, and don't accuse me of being a reactionary for saying so, because I fully recognize that you people have other compensations. You can't share our nobility, but neither do you suffer our miseries. It's been proved that all your feelings work at a different level. How can you understand why I, your master, should send a letter as complicated as a Chinese puzzle to another gentleman of similar rank? All that concerns you is the risk you run, the chance that you'll be beaten for delivering a letter you haven't even written. Yes, that risk exists, but, as a counterweight, you should keep in mind that I've been paying you punctually for several years. I don't believe you have any complaint on that score. What's more, I've already pointed out that Don Demetrio may not hit you. What happens largely depends on your own behaviour. If you faithfully follow my advice – putting aside your own interpretations – things may turn out safely. But for your own good allow me to give you a little more advice, because I haven't run out of it yet. Can I dare suggest that you wear a green wig for this evening's visit? I think your hair's a little too black. However, that's up to you. I don't want to overstep the mark or to deny you all initiative. On the other hand, wearing a green wig has its own risks, particularly in these parts. People could take you for a Martian. From what I read in the papers, there are daily more and more people who firmly believe in such marvels. Especially in these rustic regions. They've destroyed traditional mysteries, but have invented others, more in keeping with the times in which we live. Fashions, Bautista. Who was it said fashion reigns, even in crime? Fashions change, my friend, but fundamentals remain. I seem to recall this is the theme I raise in the second part of my letter. "Are *ranae* fundamental, my dear Count?" Let's now suppose that, in spite of all my precautions, Don Demetrio manages to decipher the six words of this question. Six words in minute handwriting, don't forget, with additional strokes for m's and n's. In other words, let's suppose the Count manages to read: 'areramaefumdamemtalmydearcoumt?' Oh yes, it's enough to make you die laughing! The extra stroke on the n in *ranae* – the Latin for frogs, Bautista – completely changes the meaning of the question. "Good heavens!" exclaims Don Demetrio, arching his eyebrows, "What's this that devious conspiratorial Marquis, whom I thought dead a long time ago, is asking me? Has he come back from the grave to plague me with trivial questions, like whether or not *rami* are fundamental? – getting his Latin plurals wrong, moreover." Nevertheless, the poor man will rack his brain, trying to come up with an answer, because the question isn't easy. What, Bautista, would be your answer? Do you think that *rami* – the Latin for branches, Bautista – are fundamental? You shrug your shoulders, naturally. A gesture men should be deeply ashamed of! Let's try to make an effort, let's analyse the question in depth. Are branches fundamental? At first, it seems not. Branches lack independence. They can only be born from a trunk, a tree, that is. But from another point of view it could be said that they're fundamental, because without branches there are no leaves, and without leaves trees would lose the best of their virtues. What use would a tree without leaves be to the wayfarer, Bautista? Leaves and branches make trees luxuriant, my friend, and luxuriant trees are the hurricane's best friends. But there's a further argument in favour of the fundamentality – if you'll allow the word – of branches. Listen carefully: the seeds of new trees are contained in fruit, and fruit hangs from the branches. Without noticing, we've got into the Aristotelian theory of potentiality and actuality. Therefore, if there aren't branches, neither is there fruit to hang from them. And if there's no fruit, there are no seeds which, tomorrow, can be the origin of new trees. Let's take an oak, for example, my favourite tree. In this oak's acorn another potential oak is already living. Do you follow me? Any one branch of this oak is fundamental, because without that branch there'd be no acorns, and without acorns there'd be no oak-woods. What? What are you trying to say, Bautista? That the acorns of ordinary oaks are always bitter. That acorns from holm-oaks are better? Don't be such a stickler, don't flaunt your village background. I'm just giving an example. Don't be so faithful to a word's specific meaning. Be a little more imaginative. As it happens, when we speak of trees, we may be encompassing much more. Tom Thumb's more than a mere child lost in the wood, he's willpower resolutely trying to find a way. Anyway, whatever you call them and even if holm-oaks produce sweeter acorns, my admiration for oak-trees still stands. Strong, well-intentioned giants, with a unisexual flower. The oak, my dear Bautista, is a stimulating tree, even though its longevity reminds us how fleeting our own lives are. That – drawing a rather fine point – is all I have against them. Who can plant an oak or a holm-oak without at the same time thinking of the brevity of his own life? Where will we be, and our stupid letters, and our titles, and our friendly frogs, when that tree we plant today brings forth its first acorns? Can we accept, without rebelling, that this same tree's acorns will provide food for herds of happy pigs when we've been dead for many years? Well, let's drop such digressions and get back to the matter in hand. Sometimes I get the impression that I talk too much without managing to say everything. We were discussing the Count's confusion, trying to decide if branches are fundamental or not. And perhaps, by dint of reflecting on this question,

I'm beginning to suspect that, availing myself of a fairly common literary device, I'm trying to discover how genuine is this liking for the colour green that he's always boasted about. I'll explain myself: leaves, green in spring and summer, go yellow in autumn and die in winter. Nevertheless, when people think about trees, they always imagine them green. So the Count's reasoning will go more or less like this: "Leaves are green. Green is my favourite colour. Leaves are born on branches. Branches, therefore, are fundamental, at least for me, because they provide the green I love." Isn't this a thrilling game, Bautista? But let's not count our chickens before they're hatched. It may be that Don Demetrio's reasoning will take another track. Let's suppose that the Count – who mistrusts his own shadow, as I've said before – smells a rat. He just can't understand why, after twenty years' silence, I should come back to life and ask precisely him whether or not branches are fundamental. He turns the matter over, he studies the pros and cons, he re-reads the letter and finally notices that all the n's and m's have got an extra stroke. He could find this out from the simplest words – the most difficult to disguise. Words like, for example, the copulative conjunction nor (mor in the letter) or the adverbs no (mo in the letter) or never (mever). "Good Lord!" – he'll shout, striking his brow and thinking himself the world's most intelligent man – "This devilish Marquis, whom the devil take, is trying to drive me mad! He's written *ramae* instead of *ranae*!" And here at last he comes up against a genuine big mystery: "Are *ranae* fundamental, my dear Count?" Don't be coarse, Bautista, stop snorting. And stop shaking your head, as if thanking heaven. Don't think it's all going to be plain sailing from now on. Far from it. The Count will go on doubting. It's not going to be easy to find an answer to the new question either. I told you

earlier that Don Demetrio's not a very learned man. First
of all he'll try to find out what he should understand by
fundamental, to establish a safe starting point. He'll
decide he needs to resort to the dictionary to ascertain
the official definition. Fundamental, he will then read,
is what pertains to the foundation. Foundation: the sup-
porting member of a wall or structure; base; that upon
which anything is founded. "What have frogs got to do
with buildings?" – he will ask himself – "What have they
got to do with the foundation of things?" But he'll end
up realizing, if only vaguely, that the adjective fundamental is also applied to things considered necessary. In this
sense, air is fundamental, because it's necessary. Once
having reached this point, Don Demetrio will plant the
question in the following form: "Are frogs necessary?"
The unhappy Count's doubts will then reach their peak.
Don't smile, Bautista, because progress is impossible
without doubt. Anyone who doesn't doubt at first will
be unable to arrive at the truth. So, instead of mocking
the Count's tribulations, put yourself in his place and
try to reply to the question: Are frogs fundamental or
necessary? Again, you shrug your shoulders: you're
incorrigible! You've taken no notice of my recent warning. Your class are all alike. You stir things up, submit
the most serious problems for our consideration and
demand immediate, clear solutions. But when its your
turn to reply, all you do is shrug your shoulders. All right
then! Once again, it's I who'll try to reveal the unknown.
It's not the gentleman's role to throw a stone and then
to hide. Are frogs fundamental? To start, we'll overlook
those glow-worm-devouring frogs we mentioned earlier.
It's not even worth bearing them in mind. We'll limit
ourselves to the ordinary, edible frog, which most
abounds in these latitudes. Are edible frogs fundamental? To arrive at a proper answer, let's follow the bio-

logical development of these animals, step by step. We'll go back to the beginning. When they emerge from their eggs – because, like chickens, frogs are hatched from an egg – these grotesque creatures have neither eyes nor mouth. They don't even have an anus. All they can boast of are sketchy gills. Obviously, the baby frog can't be considered fundamental. But let's give time some time, let's move forward a few days. The young frog lives on top of the mucus surrounding the spawn. The gills have begun to show on both sides of the head. He still doesn't have a mouth, but an adhesive organ, which lets him attach himself to aquatic plants, begins to sprout beneath the chin. Internal gills start replacing the external ones and a mouth, with several rows of teeth, appears. The adhesive organ disappears and the animal, thanks to a tail with a dorsal and ventral fin, can now swim. At this stage of life he's called a tadpole. Can a tadpole be said to be fundamental? I don't know what you think, Bautista, but it seems to me, no. Suffice it to give an example: insignificant men – that is, non-fundamental ones – are pejoratively called tadpoles. However, don't let's rush to conclusions, let a few more days go by. The tadpole, like a comet with a tail, loafs about the liquid firmament of the pond. His four legs arrive, first the back and then the front. Gills and tail slowly disappear. The young frog occupies land and can, at last, think of itself as an adult. Nevertheless, water goes on being the necessary basis of its life. Water is where it lays its eggs and where, in times of danger, it finds refuge. It also finds rest, peace and love in water. It has now reached its majority. But can it be considered fundamental? Control yourself, Bautista, repress your yawns. Try to disguise your fondness for ignorance a little better or you'll end up annoying me. Let's finish analysing this point. I repeat: can adult frogs be considered fundamental? Let's go about it systematically and, as we've already chosen the edible type of frog, we'll begin by considering the question from a gastronomic point of view. Is that kind of frog essential for the catering trade? I don't honestly think so. Some restaurants, it's true, serve frogs' legs as one of their great specialities, but I don't believe these restaurants' profitability and survival depend on the inclusion of so controversial a dish on their menus. Neither that, nor any other specific culinary sophistication. Don't let's lose our sense of proportion. We mustn't be like those individuals who rave on about unforgettable cheeses and divine hams. Decadence begins the day a man becomes victim of such exaggerations. Take Heliogabalus, for example, a Roman emperor who had nightingales' tongues and ostrich brains served at his banquets. What does Heliogabalus's story tell us today? Wasn't his reign one of superstition and licentiousness? And wasn't that evil monster assassinated by his own practorian guard? So, Bautista, if men could not count on any other food I might dare to believe that frogs are fundamental. They would have been fundamental for those English children who, at the height of the industrial revolution, used to steal pigs' swill. But a lot of time's gone by since then and no one would dream of stealing food from animals today. People no longer go hungry, that old problem's been overcome. What? You say it hasn't? Can that be possible? I realize, Bautista, that sometimes – and for some things – this castle's walls are excessively high. My isolation has already gone on for too long. More and more often, I ask myself: what's happening out there? What are men up to these days? Are they still engaged in ridiculous wars? Have they finally achieved what they've been craving for thousands of years? I'd like to check all that for myself, Bautista, because, inclined to mistrust, I take increasingly less notice of what they say in the papers. I think the day of my re-encounter with the world is approaching. I don't want to die in this castle, far from everyone and out of step with my fellow men. You may understand, however, that after so many years as a recluse, I need to take some precautions before returning. That's why I think it's now time to build the first bridges and to write letters which will prepare the way for my re-encounter with those who have not ceased to be my fellow men – leaving aside questions of lineage and rank. But my twenty years of shutting myself away wasn't a whim. I assure you, Bautista, there were many important reasons. It wasn't an arbitrary decision. On the contrary, I carefully weighed up the pros and cons. "Solitude," I said to myself one day, "solitude will be my haven." And I delivered myself up to it, as an adolescent does to his first love. I thought that solitude would show me how to die, for example, and that I'd be able to see all God's majesty reflected in its mirror. I stopped being a butterfly and became an earthworm, an underground worker who must move in the dark. You're smiling, Bautista? Do you despise worms? You're wrong. Not everyone can afford to be contemptuous. In case you didn't know, I can tell you that there are few known creatures more useful than the worm. There it is, working slowly but ceaselessly. Thanks to its body's musculature, it can, without jaws or paws, hollow out long galleries in the earth. It hauls fallen leaves and rotten stalks to the back of its burrow. It spends the day eating earth, which it sends through its long digestive track. It mixes the earth with acids, salts, ferments, vitamins and hormones, and then gives it back in thin, serpentine shapes. An infinity of creatures, giving life to vegetation, are then developed. The worm, Bautista, barely has eyes. It could do little in the land of the sun. Its place is in darkness. But it takes

comfort in thinking that an undefinable greatness always
throbs where darkness reigns. I don't know whether you
can understand all this, Bautista, but I can tell you that
we – the earthworm and your master – can never be
lured again by a brilliant social life. I'll come back to my
century, that now seems beyond all doubt, but I'll return
with the meekness and wisdom of the humble hermit
after years of solitude and penance. You continue to
smile? Just as you like. This morning I feel too mag-
nanimous to put you in the stocks. Let's get back to the
frogs. In spite of everything, I don't think they can be
considered fundamental, gastronomically speaking,
which was what we were doing. God forgive me for having gone in so many circles to arrive at such a simple
solution. Now we'll move on and consider the benefit
frogs yield to agriculture. Can it be said that they're fundamental in this field? Can it be asserted that frogs are
the foundation upon which agriculture is built? That
seems excessive to me. It's true they render valuable service to the countryman, I don't want to be unfair. But I
don't think we should exaggerate. With all the will in
the world, frogs can't be called fundamental. And that,
surely, will be the Count's final conclusion. Incidentally,
the Count has never worried very much about the
countryside. "Frogs are not fundamental," he will say,
"because, if they didn't exist, the world would still go on
turning." And reaching this conclusion, perhaps, this
poor man will feel as proud as Galileo must have felt,
asserting that it was the earth which circled the sun, and
not the other way round. You know very well what happens: ignorance is always ready to admire itself. Saying
that, I am, of course, referring to Don Demetrio, not to
Galileo. It's also possible that, reaching this point and
reassured by his shrewdness, he'll decide to take a break
from reading the letter. Perhaps, taking a deep breath

and a moment off, he'll concentrate his whole attention
on you. He'll wipe his hand across his brow and attempt
a smile, with no reason except to show you that he is
still standing firm in the breach and that not for the world
is he going to acknowledge defeat by my handwriting.
Realize, Bautista, that people who consider themselves
important can't allow themselves the luxury of betraying
their concern in front of others. On the contrary, they
must go out of their way to show that they are on top of
any problem. So much so that it wouldn't be surprising
if he suddenly adopted a frivolous air and started talking
about the weather, which is what we usually talk about
when a more interesting topic doesn't come to mind.
Fanning himself with the letter – another way of showing
its lack of importance for him – he'll ask you: "Doesn't
this summer strike you as being rather cool?" It's also
possible he'll ask about me, after so many years with no
news. "And what's the Marquis doing now?" – he'll say,
feigning indifference. "Has he lost all his teeth? Does he
still have any hair? Is it possible to tell me why he has
spent so long hidden away in his castle?" If this happens,
Bautista, take great care how you respond. Don't, of
course, refer to what I said about worms a moment ago.
It's not seemly for marquises to compare themselves with
earthworms. Make up a story that shows me in good
light. Refer to the fruitfulness of the contemplative life,
for example, or to the horror my century inspires in me.
"It's like this, Don Demetrio," – you can explain to him
– "my Master still has all his hair and teeth. After all,
he's somewhat younger than you, don't forget. And as
for his decision to shut himself up in his castle, he had
reasons, believe me." Let's assume that the Count wants
to know what these reasons are. We could give him hundreds of reasons, of course, but I prefer to fall back on
the episode of the leeches. A story full of symbolism.

"Twenty years ago," – you explain – "my Master was in the city. Leaving the hotel in the morning, he found himself in a street full of leeches. Horrible creatures, as long and thick as a man's arm, and a dark green colour. Some were dragging themselves along the kerb, not daring to mount the pavements. Others, however, had climbed up the lamp-posts and were hanging, motionless, by their lower suckers. My Master" (you go on explaining) "was surprised how calmly people accepted this phenomenon. Everyone seemed used to these monsters. Life proceeded normally. Shops were open, public transport was running, children were going to school, and a multitude of people was hurriedly going about its business. My Master noticed that acquaintances greeted him with resigned smiles and that everybody (old folk, adults, children) walked along the pavements as far as possible from the roadway, hugging the walls of the houses, in other words, as far as possible from the leeches. This same circumstance" (here you can explain to Don Demetrio that I've told you this story so many times that you can remember every detail) "led to a curious uncertainty among pedestrians, which would have been even funny if it wasn't for the presence of these odious creatures. On one corner, a fat man (one of those short-sighted elephants who think they own the world) bumped into a lad loaded with parcels (a chemist's assistant, thin as a rake). Following the collision, the boy fell down at the foot of a lamp-post. In the twinkling of an eye, a leech stuck its suction pad on the young lad's cheek, without the passers-by trying to prevent it. The accident had happened outside a grocer's (my Master clearly recalled that point) and two minutes later (when the boy had already lost consciousness) the shop owner approached the monster and sprinkled a large packet of salt over it. Two other men – the fat man and another – grabbed the boy by the heels and, pulling together, finally managed to free him from the suckers. You can imagine, Don Demetrio" – you emphasize, after pausing for breath – "the dismay of my Master who, horrified, witnessed this drama. He ran back to his hotel and the receptionist tried to explain things. 'I can appreciate your feeling shocked,' the receptionist said, 'but you should understand that these leeches are already part of our community. We're so used to them we'd find it hard to give them up. They arrive, engorge themselves with blood and disappear. Others return and the circle's renewed. At first they fed off a mixed diet of snails, insects and crustaceans, but now they prefer our blood.' My Master clasped his head in his hands in anguish. 'And nobody resisted?' – he exclaimed – 'Nobody protested? Nobody raised an outcry?' The receptionist shrugged. 'The worst thing,' – he went on – 'is to see them reproducing in full view. These things are hermaphrodites and don't even have a definitive sex.' Hearing this, my Master felt weak. 'You can have my room back from this moment on,' – he said – 'I'm going to leave this appalling city today.' And from then on he decided to live shut up in his castle…" That is what you must explain to Don Demetrio, Bautista. And I can assure you that, if you get the tone right, he'll listen to you without even daring to draw a breath. Perhaps, trembling, he'll ask you: "What city was that?" Don't commit yourself, say "the city", without giving any name. After all, those leeches could turn up in any city. In fact, they already have in many. You can continue: "What I want to say is that the Marquis had reasons enough for renouncing the world, retiring to his castle and avoiding the sight of so much disquiet." If you say all that, Bautista, you'll show me in a good light. I can even imagine Don Demetrio looking at you admiringly for being worthy of serving a man of my moral integrity.

Impressed by the parable of the leeches, he'll return to reading the letter with renewed enthusiasm. What will he find after my question about the frogs? I don't really remember, Bautista, but I think that, from then on, I don't even bother to put my scribbled words in order. I just put them down as they occur to me, without worrying about rules of syntax. What I can guarantee – though it pains me to tell you this – is that two minutes after recommencing the reading, he'll again feel extremely angry. What can happen next? Let's try to be precise and to put things in chronological order. First: finding that, instead of decreasing after the frog question, the letter's difficulties increase, Don Demetrio's bad temper returns. Second: he fastens his angry eyes on you, the inauspicious messenger, and is prepared to make you the target of his wrath. Third: he raises the seven-tailed whip above his head. Fourth: he notices the frogs you've just released. The question that now arises is this: given that, as we have seen, frogs are not fundamental for Don Demetrio, will they be able to make him recover his good humour? Will they be enough to make him lower his whip? Can something we don't consider fundamental restore peace and harmony? Again, we must be careful, it's no good rushing to reply without due consideration. There are two things to be considered here. One: without being fundamental, the frogs may be sufficiently important to calm the Count. Two: though not fundamental, they are his colour, green. Look where that takes us: back to the starting point! You must capture green frogs. Any other colour will be useless. In fact, I now see that frogs are not essential. We can use any animal or thing, as long as it's green. A green hen, for example, would work. Yes, yes, I know, there's no need to tell me. Green hens don't exist. And even if they did, you wouldn't be able to fit one in your pocket. Nor would they be the ideal animals to let loose in a castle's ornate drawing-rooms. Let's forget about hens, and stick to the frogs. Let's keep to the point. We won't lose time trying to foresee the reactions of a man upon whom, at any given moment, a limitless number of unforeseen forces may operate. Logic is good in reasoning, but in life it can lead us astray, because life is like a jug with two handles. We'll stick with the frogs, because better the devil you know. The worst thing, Bautista, is that it's not only the frogs. There are other problems which, up to now, we haven't taken into account. Assume, for example, that Don Demetrio receives you lying on a couch. He takes the letter you're presenting and, envisaging that reading it will take some time, he points to a chair and invites you to sit. What should you do? Accept the invitation? Refuse it with a polite, but firm smile? Here we have a lovely dilemma. I personally advise you not to sit down and to remain standing as long as the Count takes to read the letter. That, after all, is the most fitting position for servants in the presence of their superiors. There's no other position. Don't try to come out with drivel about the French Revolution, because we all know there's no revolution which, destroying one idol, doesn't put another in its place. The only revolution I worry about is that of time passing, continually reducing our chances of being happy at last. I therefore think you shouldn't sit down. But things aren't as simple as that. What if Don Demetrio feels offended by your refusal of an invitation extended in the best democratic spirit? Let's analyse this coldly, without allowing ourselves to be blinded by passion. Suppose that the Count invites someone of the same rank to sit, and this person, for whatever the reason, refuses. What would happen in that case? Nothing. It would simply mean differing attitudes between equals. But for you, a servant, to refuse the invitation, is another matter. Your refusal to sit could amount to a sort of rebellion. Because you must know, my friend, that even in humility there's the pride of not being proud. Do you understand? Men in your condition don't even have the right to reject gracious concessions. They must accept them willingly, with a smile. I doubt if social structures have changed all that much during these years. So your position's quite delicate. What to do? To refuse? To accept? To stand? To sit? Do you see how the simplest thing gets complicated as soon as one goes into it in depth? Anyway, without going into any further inquiry, it seems to me that you should adopt a half-way posture between sitting and standing, while the Count – after offering you a seat – buries himself in the letter. That would be the least compromised position. But would you be able to discover one? And even if you did, would you be able to sustain it for one or two hours, with all your muscles flexed, as if you were skiing, but without skiing? I honestly think not, especially if we take into account you've one leg shorter than the other. That's definitely going to be a complicating factor. Stay standing, Bautista, that's the best advice I can give you. Refuse the invitation, if it's made, with a nice smile. Make up some reason for not being able to sit. A strategically sited pimple might be the right approach. Or a boil, if you prefer. But remain standing, in the attitude I suggested earlier: erect, your eyes on the floor, your arms close to your sides, your hands half-clenched, with the tips of your fingers touching your trouser seams. Not with a soldier's martial air and stiffness, but with that expression – both solemn and solicitous – adopted by the *maîtres d'hôtel* of some luxury restaurants. I know, you've never graced the floor of a good restaurant, but use your imagination. Don't look at me like that, Bautista, you know me well. I'm a careful man and I can't leave the success of one of my most cherished projects to improvisation and chance. Therefore we must tie up all loose ends before you set out for Don Demetrio's castle this afternoon. Even if, as I said, life is a jug with two handles, we must study alternatives and analyse every detail. Because it sometimes happens that the key to victory lies in the most insignificant details. Enough of that. You must remain standing, while the Count tries to decipher the letter. And it's not necessary to affect the manner and expression of those *maîtres* you've never had the chance to see. It's enough if you adopt the same posture and expression you've been employing at my solitary suppers these many years. Solicitous, ready to intervene at the slightest sign that you should, but never giving me to understand that your presence is indispensable. You know how to do that well, Bautista. You do your job of butler wonderfully well. Seeing you close to the table – enveloped in your enormous silence and, at one and the same time, so near and yet so distant from my problems – I can assure you that, on more than one night, I've been on the point of asking you to sit down beside me to share the supper and to laugh along with me. "Perhaps," – I said to myself on these occasions – "he feels as lonely as I do. Maybe he too has troubles he wants to tell me about." Was I wrong to think that? Be frank, Bautista, because assuredly you are as much of woman born as I. Haven't you sometimes felt alone? Do you know what it is to be alone? Have you – like me – felt the over-riding need to lean out of this castle's battlements and to proclaim your loneliness to the four quarters of the land? Ah, there's no need to reply. That tear you're trying to retrieve with the tip of your tongue is more eloquent than a hundred speeches. But you, my good friend, haven't even got a Count to whom you can send ridiculous letters. Your former friends – if you ever had any – can't even read. For them to understand what you require of them, you'd have to hit them over the head with a hammer. Here we have a curious paradox, Bautista: to make our fellowmen understand our loneliness and helplessness, we have to wallop them. Don't you agree this contradiction explains the violence of our time? Don't you think that a strange form of inverted love throbs behind so many blood-red clouds? But let's stop philosophizing. As someone said, philosophy is only a hole opened up in the clouds. We'll come back to earth. I don't know if I mentioned this earlier, but when you deliver the letter to the Count, request him not to disfigure the sender's name, when he's tearing open the envelope, as so often happens. I want him to be able to read my name immediately. It would be a shame if, after so much effort on my part, Don Demetrio didn't know it is I precisely who am the sender. Of course, the letter's being delivered by you, my servant, but I don't want it to be you who has to explain who the sender is. That would seem to me as humiliating as going up to a stranger in the street and confessing our loneliness and telling him we need his love. I want Don Demetrio to read my name on the envelope and then to draw his own conclusions. Anyway, you're known throughout the district. Everybody, including the Count himself perhaps, knows you work in this castle. Maybe Don Demetrio will relate you with me, without having to read the sender's name. But the truth is, Bautista, I don't rely too much on people's memory, not even the memory of those who shared our better days. The faintest ink is worth more than the best memory. So don't be surprised if I'm mistrustful. It's most likely nobody remembers the Marquis of W, once so famous. Because I was famous, Bautista. More than you'd imagine. My eccentricities were the talk of the town. Men feared me, women loved me. Indispensable at functions. "How can the party begin without the Marquis?" my hosts would wail. "How tell the orchestra to strike up the first bars of the waltz, if he's not here?" "How unveil our garden's illuminated fountain?" And so on for many years. But one day the decline set in. Who knows what adverse forces were unleashed that evening? I remember I was explaining an amusing episode, of which I'd been the recent protagonist, to the Duchess of K. I finished my story and the Duchess, instead of rewarding me with one of those fascinating smiles, which I'd been accustomed to till then, frowned and looked across the room. Nevertheless, a few minutes later, the treacherous thing laughed when Baron J – a bit of an upstart, half my age – was recounting some stupidity about something which hadn't the slightest interest, of course. You understand what I'm trying to say? Today, after so many years, I still think that incident signalled the beginning of my decline. I went on attending various gatherings, but I realized that my star was increasingly on the wane. I wanted to persuade myself that it was all my imagining, but in the end I chose to exit discreetly from the stage. Since the world's against my continuing to be the first – I thought – I'll withdraw. And that's what I did. I shut myself up in this castle. I realized that the sign of the times was different and I knew how to adjust. I didn't wish to go on offering battle to my young rivals and to run the risk of fresh defeats. I can tell you that, for the first few days of my confinement, I continued to believe that someone – some good friend, some well-loved mistress – would come to rescue me. But nobody did. They calmly allowed me to become fossilized. So I stayed within these four walls, not even giving anyone the chance to see me on the battlements, looking nostalgically at the countryside. Human glory's not worth a fig, Bautista. But I still hang on to a few memories, no one can deprive me of them. What's more, I have enormous compensations. Many nights, while you're asleep, I lean out of some window or other, contemplate the firmament and journey through the stars. During the day, without opening the curtains, I take refuge among my insect books, from which I've learnt so much. I don't have to tell you, Bautista, you know very well how much time I spend reading. Don't shake your head. Here below, insects form another starry world. You'll find as many marvels in a beehive as in a galaxy. And bees aren't the only ones. Look at mayflies, for example. Go out into the garden one sunset and sit beside the pond. Thousands of mayflies. Learn the lesson these minute creatures teach. Their maturity lasts only a few hours. They can't even permit themselves the luxury of thought. They're forced to act. They have no mouth, or only a rudimentary one. They even lack a digestive system as such. They don't need to eat. In an instant they are going to consume the energy they've been storing up for the three or four years they've spent as active larvae below the pond's waters. Everything was measured millions of years ago, Bautista. Evening falls and the mayflies take off in flight. A dense swarm. Those who are lucky enough to find a female separate her from the group and they couple in silence. No superfluous words, no sighs, not one recrimination. No promises. Life, which has just begun, is already ending for them. Night closes in and the female, loaded with eggs, plunges into the waters of the pond and deposits her eggs under a submerged stone. She never reappears. Her companions, their wings outspread, fall in their thousands. Everything is over. But the miracle of the continuity of the species is under way. What do you think of this supreme example, Bautista? Don't you think those insects give a sovereign lesson to men such as I,

who will disappear without trace? Pay a little more attention to the seething world around you, and you'll grow
wiser. And if you don't like insects, look upwards.
Observe the bat's zigzag flight. Don't unfairly condemn
its ugliness. Think that many of these creatures bravely
confront sunlight so as to be able to fly alongside emig-
rating swallows. The emigration ends, but their ugliness
continues. Aren't you stirred by the simplicity of these
creatures, who think the swallow's beauty contagious?
So you see, Bautista: without leaving this castle, I have
my own marvellous repertory. Therefore it's even more
deplorable that I feel alone. Especially these last few
months. Loneliness begins to hurt, my friend, and sometimes I think I run the risk of going mad. The moment
comes when the solitary man shuts his beautiful insect
book and clutches at desperate letters, though knowing
in advance he'll never get a kind reply. That's the reason
– I don't recall if I've already given you another one – I
prefer my letter to be incomprehensible. If they don't
reply, I'll think it's because they can't understand me.
But enough of lamentation. Don't yield to nostalgia. The
weakest goes to the wall. Where were we? Ah yes, we
were talking about how famous I once was. Perhaps it
was unfair of me not to depend on Don Demetrio's memory. Maybe the old rogue still remembers me. Just in case,
don't say it's I who am writing. Let him read the sender's
name. Let him mouth my name. "Is it possible?" he'll
ask himself, the letter trembling in his hands. "Is that
old fox still alive?" It's time you understood what this
letter means to me, Bautista. It means neither more nor
less than my resurrection into the world of the living. A
resurrection I've decided to declare unilaterally. Because
it no longer bothers me not to be the first in my group,
the centre of all, as I once was. All I want is to return,
and I hope to God I haven't left it too late. The only

drawback is that the dead, when they decide to be resuscitated, notice that they no longer know what to say to the living. They've lost the habit of smiling and of ordinary speech. The only language within call is the one they've learnt during years of solitude and silence. They don't know how to find another. Do you understand this as well, Bautista? The letters of the resurrected must always be illegible. We can't run the risk of letting others discover our splendid secrets. We can't allow ourselves the luxury of being clear nor, with the best will in the world, forgive the flowers for flourishing while we were away. Here we've another argument to justify my letter's illegibility. A weighty reason which, on its own, could absolve me from accusations of madness. So I'm completely relying on you, Bautista. It could even be said that I'm delivering my resurrection into your hands. Was that ten striking? Or eleven? It doesn't matter, we've plenty of time. Our preparations could well be even longer, infinitely minute and detailed. But when you leave this room, don't lose a second. Act calmly but continually, as they say. First of all, go to the pond and capture the frogs. Then go to my former steward's room and try on his green clothes. That man was more or less the same height as you. But let's go step by step, don't let's rush things. Returning to the frogs, I don't think they'll be hard to catch. Approach the pond on tiptoes and concentrate on the ones on the bank, that is, the ones nearest to hand. Don't underrate them, because they're sharp and distrustful. If you don't approach them silently, they'll jump into the water and put themselves beyond your reach. You could use one of those butterfly nets. Use the procedure you prefer. It's your responsibility. Whatever way, once you've caught them, pick them up carefully, don't squash them with those big fingers of yours. You should carry a small plastic bag with a bit of water in it. Put them inside. Then bring them here to show me. I want to see what type of frog you think the most appropriate. We'll go through the pros and cons for the last time, you dress in green, I give you the letter and you leave at once for Don Demetrio's castle. It'll take more than two hours to get there, assuming you don't loiter on the way. I don't know if it'll end up raining this afternoon. Last night they were forecasting heavy showers and this morning, from my bedroom window, I thought I saw a cloud-covered sky. It had an ashen face, as the poet said. So if it doesn't clear up, I won't even be able to fall back on the stars tonight. Anyway, take an umbrella. Don't run pointless risks. Rain's a nuisance. It's too much of a democratic phenomenon for my liking: it wets both master and servant. Some years back a subversive element, who deservedly went to prison for his pains, suggested the promulgation of a law forcing it to rain the other way round, in other words, from the ground upwards, to that it would only wet us, the ones above. By above, I mean the privileged. Do you get the point? A nonsense! A stupid suggestion which nobody took seriously and which even annoyed quite a few, because, obviously, nobody wants to go against nature. And not only because of the inconvenience this type of rain would mean for my class, but also because, if it rained the other way round, even the most humble people would be obliged to carry umbrellas upside down. You're smiling, Bautista? Perhaps you think I exaggerate? After so many years in my service, are you still unable to tell when I'm joking? Or are you perhaps prepared to accept rain coming from the bowels of the earth, like a fountain? Anyway, as far as this afternoon's weather goes, we can't be sure. Perhaps it won't even rain from the sky downwards, which is how it's always rained, and how it will for world without end. The truth is I don't have much faith in meteorological forecasts. It only needs a little wind to drive all those clouds to the devil. What's wrong with people today, Bautista? Why are they so obsessed with cyclones and anticyclones and storms? What lies behind this devotion to isobars? I don't know why, my friend, but there seems to me something nasty about it, I suspect some odd guilt complex. People who start forest fires inspect the heavens to see how the clouds are doing. Don't you think there's a contradiction? To summarize: take an umbrella even if the sky's as clear as a bird's eye when you're ready to leave. A man with an umbrella always looks good. Your elegance won't bother me. "What's this?" people will say when they see you. "Can that distinguished-looking gentleman, dressed in green, with an umbrella like a walking-stick, be the Marquis of O's servant? Can it be possible that a gentleman, who has the luck to be served by a man of such bearing, stays shut up in his castle? What have we, his neighbours, done wrong to be deprived of a man who shows such good taste in choosing his servants?" A servant's elegance always reflects well on his master, Bautista. Carry an umbrella, because seeing you so well turned out will refresh a few memories and remind people I was the most distinguished gentleman in the district. What's more, this umbrella could render you an ancillary service. Remember that an umbrella, apart from protecting us from the rain and having a decorative purpose, can also become an excellent means of warding off an unexpected attack. Don't make a face, I'm about to explain. Earlier, I said that if the Count decides to beat you, you mustn't offer any resistance. Nor must you defend yourself, if Don Demetrio expressly orders one of his servants to strike you. But let's now suppose that you reach the castle and some servant or other opens the service door and, seeing you dressed in green, starts to laugh his head off. "Who are you?" he'll ask, doubling up. "A man or a green pepper carrying an umbrella?" I know, Bautista, I know! You're a man who's had to listen to terrible insults all your life. You'll have surely been called stupid, silly, foolish, idiotic, imbecilic, asinine and I don't know what else. A moment ago, we even considered the possibility that the Count may call you a worm, and we agreed you'd resign yourself to such an insult. I've already told you the saying: grin and bear it. But do you also have to put up with a man like yourself calling you a green pepper? Does humiliation have to go so far? Certainly not! Don't put up with that, Bautista! I earnestly entreat you! React resolutely! Vent your anger on that insolent wretch! Now do you see? The umbrella's moment has come. You can use it like a sword. Of course, you haven't the slightest idea about fencing, because that's a gentleman's activity, but here and now I'm going to give you four basic rules. Don't get worried, it's very easy. First of all, we must learn the on-guard position, the most important for the fencer. There are four lines or positions: high, low, right and left. Don't look for others because you won't find them. And, against the four attacks, which in theory can move along these four lines, you can oppose four parries, but, as each of these parries is divided by two, according to whether your hands are held with the nails showing or facing downwards, and as the same principle applies to the attack as to the parry, it means there are eight different ways of attacking and parrying, which, multiplied by the two lines, result in sixteen different combinations. Do you follow me, Bautista? Are so many numbers making you dizzy? Don't get disheartened, it's not as hard as it seems at first. Watch me and see how I attack this vase. Imagine I'm holding a sword in my hand. Decisiveness counts. The attack is the hit or cut you use to try to wound your enemy, and you can choose among various kinds: straight-thrust, time-hit, stop-hit, riposte, indirect riposte, compound riposte, counter-riposte and lunge. I think I've told you all of them. Always bear in mind that decisiveness doesn't mean being careless, so, as long as the fight lasts, keep a cool head. Don't for a moment lose your composure. If you decide it's best to attack, you must advance your right foot and, immediately after, your left. If, on the other hand, you decide you should fall back, you should do the opposite: withdraw first the left foot and then the right, keeping your feet on the floor all the time and without dropping your guard. Persuade yourself that your umbrella is really a sword and that, using such an arm, you are allowed any circular motion, as long as it's done without dishonouring your adversary, however roused your blood. Come on, Bautista! Take heart! Once more I see you growing pale! Can it be possible you think yourself incapable of doing something so simple? You prefer using the umbrella as if it were a stick? Well, do what you think best. Don't abide by any rules and give that insolent creature as many umbrella-blows as you like. Break his head for him. You are, after all, a plebeian, and it was silly of me to think you'd be able to conduct yourself like a gentleman. You do realize, Bautista? Things haven't changed very much all these years. Everything's the same as when I left it. Peasants go on being peasants, democracy hasn't rearranged anything. I'll leave my castle and find the world turning on the same old axis, however much a few contemplative romantics may believe that men can now grow old with more dignity. Tell me, my friend, who can change the colour of loneliness by popular plebiscite? What system of government and what new social model can bell death's cat? It's quite clear, Bautista: there's no point giving man the sky, because he wasn't born with wings. Their most real problems will always be solved by men alone with themselves, before the mirror of their consciences. The echo of the merry din reaching even the solitary's small room can never redeem him from that great commitment. To expect anything else would be a sin of pride. But let's go back to the matter in hand. We'd decided you were incapable of using the umbrella as if it were a sword. All right, use it, then, as if it were a stick. Give free rein to your instincts and don't stop until that scoundrel asks your pardon on his knees. But don't let yourself be softened by entreaties. Take him by the ear and command him to lead you to the Count's study without further delay. And while you're proceeding along the castle corridors, don't allow him the slightest hesitation. Remember you're on enemy territory. He can easily trick you. Suppose that this servant, jealous of his master's privacy, decides to go round in circles, never getting to your destination. I'm not meaning you, Bautista, but everyone knows that servants' sutbborn intransigence is usually more fanatical than their masters'. If he is meekly left to lead, you may spend the whole afternoon going down passages, mounting sumptuous staircases, crossing enormous reception rooms. Don Demetrio's castle is vast and you won't be able to know if you're going through the same place twice. So, act without ceremony. Place yourself behind your guide and prod him with your umbrella. Let him be aware that he may get another umbrella-blow to the head when least expected. As soon as he shows you the Count's study, say goodbye with a resounding smack, just in case he took you out of your way. Then wipe all trace of anger from your face and knock on the door with your knuckles. Ask: "Do I have your permission?" And when Don Demetrio concedes this, gently you push open the door, carefully closing it behind you. Move four steps forward, bow and hand over the letter. Move back four steps to where you were and wait. I say four, but, as you may realize, that's merely an example, because it may be that the Count's settee is further from the door and you'll have to advance fourteen, twenty or forty steps. I advise you to mind your manners particularly in these first moments, because they're the most delicate. The Count, with a careless gesture, may motion you to withdraw, before even opening the envelope. You mustn't move, however. If he insists, explain your immobility. "My master, the Marquis of Q," – tell him – "particularly wants me to stay by Your Excellency while you are reading the epistle I have just delivered. My master has been too long removed from the world to be able to be indifferent to the reaction that a letter of his – the first he has written in twenty years – may awake in a gentleman of your rank. A reaction that I must then pass on to him, including its finer shades. It could be," – you go on to explain to him – "that this letter is even a kind of test, so that my master can then decide whether or not it's worth while returning to this century." Bautista, I'm convinced that if you offer him this explanation, Don Demetrio will willingly allow you to continue in his presence. Your green clothes, so gratifying to his senses, will help things still more. I'm only referring to those early moments, of course. We've already seen what his later reactions could be. What I must warn you of now is that, precisely during those early moments, there's the risk I touched on previously, but we didn't look at it too closely. I'm referring to Don Demetrio's fondness for testing his interlocutor's mettle and ability to react, with random questions when least expected, a fondness he's surely kept all these years. Earlier, I used agrarian reform as an example, and it was quite clear what your opinion about that should be. But now imagine that, instead of

choosing the problem of *latifundia*, he selects something else. University massification, for example, which
the papers are now so full of. "Are you a supporter of
the *numerus clausus*, Bautista?" Worse still: let's suppose that the Count wants to know what's the worth of
those who opt for withdrawal and the contemplative life
in these times of political agitation and mass demonstra-
tions. In that case, his question would be more or less
this: "Do you believe, Mr Whoever-you-are, that the contemplative life is truly profound?" Be careful then how
you respond, my faithful friend, because there's more in
the answer than meets the eye. What Don Demetrio will
really want to know is your opinion of my decision to
stay shut up in this castle. Perhaps he hopes to hear my
own servant accuse me of egotism or cowardice. Maybe
he wants to pump you for something he can then use
against me. Take care not to fall into his trap. "Sir," –
you can reply without committing yourself – "we are
going through one of the worst crises known to history.
We find ourselves between two eras. One, which wants
to take its leave fighting up to the last moment to keep
its communal traditions. Another which, come what
may, wants a fresh start." Possibly the Count will be
satisfied with that reply. But it's also possible he'll want
more explanation. "I agree with everything you say," –
he will, in this case, insist – "but tell me now what you
think of the contemplative life. And don't beat about the
bush." You, however, must go on being ambiguous. "The
clash between these two eras," – you reply – "has been
harsh and has led to uneasiness and uncertainty in
thousands of souls." Don Demetrio gets impatient: "All
right, but what does all that mean to you precisely?" he
inquires, clenching his fists. Don't let yourself be intimi-
dated, don't get sidetracked, Bautista. Say to him: "It
means that the contemplative life is as real today as it

was yesterday. The world, my Lord, goes on needing the contemplative's silent, hidden presence." Don Demetrio's brow is smooth again and he starts to laugh. "You're a model servant," he says, "no doubt about it. Utter fidelity! All that harangue was to justify your master's position, running away from his obligations twenty years ago and shutting himself up in his castle, while we ran risks, clamouring for justice in broad daylight. It's no good the Marquis trying to deceive me. Nobody can take me in. I well know that your master's life hasn't been as contemplative all this time as you'd like us to think, far from it. Old birds are not caught with chaff. I admit that, for twenty years, he's given up leaving his castle, but has the Marquis also been able to give up a certain type of visit all this time? Answer me truthfully, Mr What's-your-name, because you're his servant and servants are always in on the secret. Of course not! I have my own information: the Marquis has been pretty active on a fairly regular basis. More exactly, every weekend for the last year, your master has been exemplifying La Rochefoucauld's maxim: Love, like fire, cannot exist without continual movement. Yes, yes, a lot of movement! Or do you think that any man who boasts of his manhood could maintain his passive attitude in Baroness O's company? So don't give me your contemplative life! None of your uneasy, uncertain souls! Your master's a knowing old dog." You see where the shots are coming from now, Bautista. But don't be put out. If the Count takes that line, which is more than possible, limit yourself to a confused smile. Act as if the revelation of my flirtations has made you feel a bit ashamed. Initially keep quiet and don't try to contradict him. And don't try to justify my bad behaviour, or to deny the facts, because we wouldn't come out on top. The Count must still have his own network of informers and it may be that he has more than one proof of my fling with the Baroness. He may even know that her recent abortion had a lot to do with one of our last secret meetings. But his attitude of tacit recognition of the facts mustn't be allowed to prolong itself indefinitely. Fairly soon, you should adopt the expression of one who, while admitting an element of truth in the accusations levelled against him, wants to put things in perspective. There must not be any misunderstandings. Raise your eyes from the floor, stop blushing and try to make Don Demetrio understand that my clandestine meetings with the Baroness did not alleviate my loneliness for a single second. If anything, they made it more acute. I'm not talking for the love of it, Bautista. You know Doña Brigida. Can you imagine a man like me being able to feel really at home with such a woman? I assure you that all she could give me was a moment's satisfaction, and not always that. Nothing more. That instant over, my sadness was greater than before. Loneliness always returned, like a bird with outspread wings. I could add, so you'll really be convinced, that I even began feeling an unpleasant aftertaste of disappointment each time that she, the fleeting tremor flown, snorted and turned her back on me. It was quite useless, then, in a desperate effort to redeem her, to talk about distant violins. You see the sort of relationship it was, Bautista, my friend. You know that I don't usually speak badly of women, but I can assure you that to tell the truth about some of them turns out to be even worse than slander. Doña Brigida has more than once reminded me of the praying mantis, that fine mysterious creature which, after coupling, devours the male. Once, putting my finger in her mouth, I said: "Here I am." She, instead of taking my invitation as a joke, viciously fastened her teeth on it. A frightful bite! She didn't let my finger go until she saw I was about to faint. I'm still asking myself: what

was that woman trying to prove that day? Was she showing me that she still had sufficient strength to tear me to
pieces with her teeth after our laborious amorous
encounter? To let me know I wasn't sufficiently virile to
leave her exhausted? Watch out for that smile of yours,
Bautista, don't try to minimize things, or to come out
with one of your silly stories, and don't try to justify that
maneater. I don't believe in that business of "loving you
so much, I want to eat you." Because Doña Brigida isn't
in love with me, for one thing. Never was. All I'll concede
is a foolish passion for love itself, because that, more or
less, is what happens with all lovers over forty. I assure
you that the most important thing for all those women
is to prove to themselves that they're still capable of passionate love. But don't let's waste any more time on the
Baroness. We'll get back to where we were: if the Count
elects to be ironic about the genuineness of my contemplative life, make him understand that going to bed once a
week with Doña Brigida, almost by medical prescription,
doesn't mean I'm playing a double game, far from it. Tell
him that my loneliness has always been intact, untouched
by that very superficial erotic play. Right. We'll file that.
The Count accepts the validity of your argument, lights
his long meerschaum pipe and goes back to reading.
You're again silent, closely watching his reactions, not
missing a single detail, because when you get back
tonight or tomorrow I want you to confirm, point by
point, what I'm now conjecturing. Oh yes! I can just see
him. There he is, the cretin, stretched out on his red
velvet couch, gasping like a fish out of water. He's holding the letter in his right hand and, with his left, he occasionally strokes his temple's little blue vein, which is
dangerously knotted. His uneasiness is growing. The
sudden arrival of a simple letter has shown him that not
even he is immune to madness, that's how life goes.

Everything's begun to crumble around him. He wants to clutch at a string of commonplaces, but the excuses he finds have no consistency. His bourgeois convictions are worthless. He, who believed himself on top of everything! Pay close attention, Bautista! The Count's on the point of breaking into tears and not far short of falling on his knees and begging forgiveness for sins he's never committed! Good God! And what if I'd no right to torment him in this way? Am I being too cruel? Ought we to open the eyes of those who've always lived happily short-sighted? Anyway, Bautista, if the Count breaks into tears, don't go up to him. Don't try to comfort him. Let him enjoy himself, because there's a certain voluptuousness in tears. But don't drop your guard. Be prepared for whatever problem unexpectedly arises. The frogs, for example. Don't for a moment forget that you're carrying them in your pocket. Suppose they begin to croak while Don Demetrio's weeping. A possibility we've already partially dealt with. What can you do then? Use your imagination, my dear friend. For example, you could pretend it's you who's croaking. Don't reveal your treasure yet. The frogs will lose most of their efficiency if their appearance doesn't take the Count completely by surprise. "Actually," – you say, without attaching any importance to it – "it was I who croaked. I sometimes do it without realizing. You should know that I was born in a humble hovel, alongside the pond, and on many nights during the first years of my life I was lulled to sleep by the song of frogs. It was, in fact, my first language and, without my being able to repress them, childhood's sweet sounds come to my throat even today." The Count, who stopped crying when he heard the frogs, licks away his last tear. "Wasn't it Cicero who said," – you continue, to give even more credibility to your words – "that a child's soul is like a mirror in which nature is reflected?

And don't the Chinese maintain that memories have more aroma than lilac in full bloom?" The Count smiles, admiring your erudition. But now suppose that, while you're telling him this, the frogs – who lack the gift of timing – croak again. What should you do? Above all, don't let it throw you off balance. Don't be ashamed of having been caught out in a lie. Remember that we're living in times in which people publicly boast of much worse vices. It would be a good solution if you could say you're a ventriloquist and therefore able to speak and croak at the same time. But that would complicate things. It seems to me you should tell the truth, simply and calmly. Without beating about the bush. Excuse yourself for having said it was you who had croaked and immediately, before he's time to make an objection, take the frogs from your pocket and lay them at his feet, like an offering. I'm sure that will move him profoundly. "What's this you've brought me?" – he'll ask. "Can they be frogs?" You nod your head. "Yes, Excellency," you can reply. "A couple of frogs captured on his Lordship's estate. The best I could find. His Lordship would feel most honoured if Your Excellency, in accepting them, took them as a sincere expression of the esteem which Your Excellency merits." Hearing this, Don Demetrio will flush with pleasure and, to show how happy he is, he'll perhaps try to stroke the batrachians, who will be gleaming like two throbbing emeralds on the darker green of the carpet. He won't manage to, because the frogs will hop out of reach. It may be that he'll then ask you to imprison them in an urn he'll point to. You obey. Put the frogs in the urn and hand it to him with another bow. Don Demetrio, pressing the urn to his breast, will lie down on his couch again. "How long can they stand being inside there?" – he'll ask, fascinated by the small animals' hypnotic stare. Say whatever you think. Two, three, four, five or even six years. "So long?" the Count will exclaim, with a shiver. His hands will tremble and the urn will be on the point of falling. To prevent that accident, you must take the urn from him and put it back on the mahogany commode. "The frogs from his Lordship's ponds are famous for their longevity," – you reply – "But should they die before their time, their marvellous green will still survive them a few years, for Your Excellency's pleasure and delight. That is characteristic of our batrachians and is their chief virtue." Don Demetrio will feel even more admiration. He'll finally appreciate the magnitude of my gift. A green that outlives death. A joy for ever, as the poet says. Even if they were possible, would such priceless gifts ever be given? Because the butterflies we see fluttering among the flowers are not the same as those we inspect in the collector's display cabinet, pierced by the cruel pin. Death puts out their wings' magic gleam. And there's that other marvellous insect, the gadfly. Have you ever seen a gadfly? Its eyes are coloured with spots, specks and strips of brilliant shades which run the gamut of the spectrum. Microscopic structures of the tegument break up the light rays, dispersing them in different wavelengths. What happens when the gadfly dies? All that beauty disappears in an instant. The eye's tegument contracts, the structures alter, the colours fade away. The moral that follows from that sudden collapse is clear: all those who want to enjoy the beauty of the gadfly's eyes – multi-coloured like Gothic stained glass – must also be prepared to put up with its stings. A dead gadfly doesn't annoy, but neither does it delight. You notice how much wisdom I can find in my books, Bautista? But to get back to frogs: you must convince Don Demetrio that their green colour will persist after they've died. It's not true, of course, but you must tell him so and, what's more, make him firmly believe it. We mustn't bother about what happens later, when the frogs die, because all that interests us is that this poor man, drained by my handwriting, gets sufficient encouragement to go back to reading the letter, with renewed hope. We're approaching the culminating moments of your mission. When the Count, sighing – but comforted by the presence of the two green frogs – continues trying to decipher my letter, you must exercise your vigilance even more. Try not to let a single detail escape you. Scrutinize the slightest peculiarities in his expression, the changing radiance of his regard, the mobile line of his eyebrows...Even observe the rhythm and depth of his breathing. Remember that I'm expecting an exhaustive report. I'll ask you everything that occurs to me and even more. All right, Bautista, don't start raising your eyebrows again, I know you well and I know what you're thinking! Why such thoroughness? you're wondering once more. The answer's obvious. I've already told you this letter may mean my resurrection into the world of the living, now I'm going to explain it another way. Listen carefully and stop wrinkling your nose: the letter you'll take to Don Demetrio this afternoon is an experiment. And whether we send similar letters to the region's other chatelains depends upon this experiment's success. There are many of us in this country who live locked away in our respective fortresses, but it was surely I who gave the others the idea that they could find a selfish salvation, each alone in his castle. This responsibility now frightens me, Bautista. I started thinking about this a few days ago. I also thought about the effectiveness of my own incarceration. Last night, precisely, I was plagued by the following question: are such medieval remedies still possible? Don't we have common problems and, even though we hate the idea, aren't our castles interlocking? Aren't we all joined by the same kind of madness? Pay close attention to what I'm saying, my friend, because not even I myself really understand what I mean. I'm afraid I'm involving myself in contradictions. Because these reasonable doubts about the justice of my confinement and my renunciation of the world have little to do with the moral of my story about the leeches – a story which, of course, I never experienced – or with my indifference to what happens outside, while I leaf through my beautiful books. Might it be true that the most sincere are those who contradict themselves? Well whatever, Bautista, I have a premonition that this letter is going to mark an important milestone in my life. That's why I'm so interested in knowing point by point all the Count's reactions to my approach. Who knows, all this could be the dawn of a new stage for Humanity! A stage which will bury all egotisms. Do you see, my friend? You, with your limited parochial vision, are to become the keystone of a great project: universal fraternization! Don't you feel proud? Aren't you prompted to kiss my hands and to swear by your loved ones that you will even go beyond the call of duty in carrying out your mission? My dear Bautista, this afternoon you will become a new Mikhail Strogoff, a spirited Czar's messenger, ready to confront the greatest danger in delivering the confided message. Faced with such a fine, noble mission, the risk that the Count, in spite of the green frogs and everything else, may take an ash to one's ribs, means nothing. Because, if you want me to be honest, it's possible the frogs won't be a strong enough talisman to free you from a flogging. Particularly bearing in mind that the Count may be accompanied by his wife, in which case you couldn't resort to them. If that is the case – I've already told you, but I'm doing so again – forget about the frogs. It would be very dangerous to take them out of your pocket in the Countess's presence,

I must insist on that. A squeal from that distinguished lady, and the Count will hurl himself on you, dagger in hand. Remember then: if Doña Beatriz is there, don't take out the frogs, or move an inch. Keep your provocative buttocks in check. I've good authority for saying Don Demetrio is as jealous as ever. Be motionless as long as it's necessary. Your eyes on the floor. Whatever happens. Even if the Count's called away on urgent business, leaving you alone with Doña Beatriz. In which case, the situation becomes extraordinarily complicated. As you can imagine, my dear friend, I couldn't care less what happens between the Countess and you. It wouldn't be the first time a well-born lady felt attracted to – and was even seduced by – a peasant's beautiful brutishness. But this, apart from moral considerations, becomes a source of serious complications. History tells us so. We've the example of Faustina who, although a Roman empress, fell hopelessly in love with a gladiator. You're smiling again? You find the comparison amusing? I agree you've little of the gladiator, but neither is Doña Beatriz as beautiful as that lady must've been. The ratio, therefore, remains. We can assume that the provocation was Faustina's, although the chronicles don't say. Without doubt, it was she who roused the gladiator. And history could repeat itself. Like all fat women, Doña Beatriz is fairly bashful, but, behind a curtain of modest demeanour, she's capable of hiding an overwhelming passion. Let's try to picture what could be the scene. We'll have a flashback, like in the cinema. The Count has received you in the company of his wife. You hand over the letter and he starts to read it. Unexpectedly, a servant enters and agitatedly announces the Archduke's arrival. Somewhat surprised (so high a dignitary's visit to his castle is infrequent), Don Demetrio hurries from the room to the library, where the august personage awaits him. He knows he runs a risk, leaving his wife with you, but the Archduke's visit leads him to expect some soft job or sinecure, and he doesn't hesitate to run that risk. Put another way: he prefers – in spite of his frequently manifested jealousy – an explosive adultery to losing the chance of concluding a worth-while deal. He leaves the room and closes the door behind him. You two are alone, enveloped in an awkward silence. The initiative comes from Doña Beatriz, as I said before. She sighs deeply and winks. You hold out and she persists. She sighs again, approaches you and gives you a little nudge with her hip. (A very slight nudge, almost a graze, given the width of her hips.) Well, Bautista, faced with such great provocation, what should you do? What should be your reaction? Ought you to be a gentleman and to respect Don Demetrio's absence? My friend, I don't want to minimize matters: you're in an awful dilemma. Wherever you look, there are manifold dangers. Because if Doña Beatriz makes advances and you refuse them, she may feel indignant. That wouldn't be good. You know what happens in such cases. Women can forgive someone who tries to take liberties, but never the one who fails to take advantage of a favourable opportunity. So, if the Countess winks at you and you, blushing, lower your eyes, you'd be running the risk of converting her into your worst enemy. Most likely she'd turn things round and, when the Count got back, accuse you of the very sin she'd been trying to commit. "That peasant!" – she'll cry, in this event – "Will my rightful Lord allow his lawful wife to be besieged by a servant?" Such an accusation, my poor friend, would mean a death sentence. Before you could open your mouth to defend yourself, the Count's dagger would be sunk in your heart. It won't be a waste of time, then, if we look calmly at this delicate point. You have the following choice: to pick up the amorous gauntlet or not to pick it up; in other words, to flow with Doña Beatriz's current or to disabuse her from the beginning. What do you think, Bautista? In a certain way, I think it would be better if your responded to the woman's advances. Why not? What can you lose? Forward, my dauntless Romeo! If the Countess does wink, you, without a blush, immediately respond with a passionate glance. What happens next is an enigma, because women aren't fond of logic, they run on alternating current. Perhaps, feeling herself buffeted by youi glance, Doña Beatriz will be frightened and go into reverse. But maybe she'll push ahead. Marvellous. You accept the invitation, even at the risk of the Count's returning prematurely and catching you hard at it. Do you realize, Bautista, how complicated it is whenever a man tries to foresee the future? Multiple alternatives. The first premise – giving point to all our lucubrations – is that Don Demetrio receives you in his wife's company. From then on, a fan of possibilities opens out. First possibility: Don Demetrio, summoned by urgent business, interrupts his reading of the letter and leaves the room. Second possibility: the Countess deliberately sets out to seduce you. Third possibility: you – a man, after all – accept the invitation. Fourth possibility: unlike some women, Doña Beatriz doesn't go into reverse at the last moment. Fifth possibility: the Count returns before he's expected – no clanking spurs in the corridor – and surprises you both heaped on the divan, trying to find the ideal position. But other situations could be postulated. For example, it might be you who, at the vital moment – because of serious moral objections or physiological impossibility – leave the Countess crestfallen. Or maybe you, Bautista, will issue the invitation to adultery, without waiting for Doña Beatriz's incitement. Anything might be expected from a man with a limp as randy as yours! Then she might accept. Or she might not. It's even possible that the incitements to love are reciprocal and synchronized, or, although reciprocal, not simultaneously manifest. Anyway, many things can happen. Don't let's tantalize ourselves any more. What I do want to make clear is that I don't care what happens between the Countess and you. I, too, had my chances and the devil knows I used them to advantage. But let's suppose without further complicating the issue that, benefitting from being alone, you and the Countess desire intercourse, and that the Count, coming back to the room, catches you in passionate coitus. That'd be the worst possible outcome. Do you imagine that the Count would have the slightest desire to go back to reading my letter after having surprised his wife in the postman's arms? I can't believe that customs will have changed so much in the last few years, Bautista. That's why I'd prefer Don Demetrio to receive you on his own. We'd save ourselves the chance of a number of additional problems and, if in a jam, you could calmly resort to freeing the frogs. When all's said and done, we still haven't considered the possibility that, sometime during these twenty years, Don Demetrio may have become a widower. It's true I haven't had news of this, and it's also true that the percentage of wives who survive their husbands is much higher than the other way round. But in Don Demetrio's case we could have the exception that proves the rule. That would be the best thing for us: a widowed Count. You know what they say: a childless widower leads the happiest life. Perfect. Let's suppose now that things are as we want them to be: let's suppose that Don Demetrio, a contented widower, receives you on his own. Hardly have you entered the room, when he leaps up from his couch and runs to meet you. He knows you're my servant as soon as he sees you. "God be praised!" – he exclaims.

"Give me that letter I've been waiting so long for!" You hand it over and he begins to wave it above his head, as if it were a little flag. To justify his jubilation – which you find a little hard to understand – he explains that the letter puts an end to twenty years of resentment and isolation. At least, he hopes so. "But," – he goes on to brag – "it had to be your master who took the first step, because he knows I was the offended party and he the offender." Don't ask me now, Bautista, what the offence was. I don't remember, too much time has gone by. Maybe there was some difference of opinion between the Count and myself. Perhaps there was some woman. Doña Beatriz, perhaps, but the details have gone with the wind. But Don Demetrio is a spiteful chap and if there really was something between us, he'll not have forgotten it. I know him fairly well. Men like him may lose their teeth but never their memory, so, during all these years he'll have been expecting my excuses. Note what can happen now, things are getting more and more involved. Don Demetrio takes the letter and, reading the sender's name, rubs his hands. He remembers me very well and thinks that, at last, he's going to get complete satisfaction for a longstanding wrong. His honour is going to be satisfied. He opens the envelope, unfolds the letter and sighs. His nostrils imperceptibly dilate, his eyes gleam. But what can he read? Nothing, apart from the heading. The rest gibberish. He thinks the fault's his – ignorant people always start off doubting themselves – and for an hour he struggles to locate in the letter the longed-for apology. Finally he gives up. His teeth grind. He begins to see everything clearly. The calligraphic chaos, he thinks, has only one objective: to humiliate him even further. The old affront (because I now recall that there was, in fact, an argument over a skirt) resurfaces, reinforced by twenty years' silence. He pales with anger and rage. He clenches his fists and damns my soul. He calls his servants and commands them to beat you. Perhaps, grabbing you by the collar, he prefers to take justice into his own hands. Because you, as I said before, are the unlucky messenger, and where there's no bread, let them eat cakes. If that is his reaction – or if he decides to pretend, making up some text, an eventuality we've already discussed – I don't give a fig. It's entirely his problem. But what I couldn't accept is that, giving in to the letter's difficulty at the very start, he should adopt a disdainful, pitying attitude to what is, most definitively, a gesture of good will on my part. Because my letter, Bautista – I can't recall whether I've already told you this but, if not, I'm doing so now – is above all an attempt at dialogue, and an attempt at dialogue is always a chance of love. But let's proceed. We'll imagine that Don Demetrio, after a rapid glance at the letter, sadly shakes his head. "From what I see," – he says in his horrible nasal voice – "your master, the Marquis of Q, is a hopeless case. He goes on being as eccentric as ever. Is he still washing his feet in French champagne?" That's where I want to see you in action, Bautista. Don't let me down. If the Count says that, I authorize you to make an energetic reply. Don't lose your composure, but don't mince words either. Assure him that I'm not mad. Tell him that my extravagances of yesteryear – I admit that more than once I washed my feet in French champagne – have served to make me now appreciate the superiority of a life hallowed by sobriety and meditation. "My Lord," – you can reply – "you regrettably err if you think that my master is the same man who shared so many nights of wine and roses with you. You are wrong if you think he's the same as when he seduced your two sisters and was on the point of running off with your wife, Doña Beatriz, when the marriage banns had already been published. My master is now another man. A man who's decided to regain the world's affection and esteem. If it's true he sinned, his penitence has been long and has freed him from blame. You see the colour of this suit. And you see these two frogs. He told me to put them in my pocket, because he remembered you love the colour green. Isn't that a sign of good will?" I think the Count will begin to look at you with fresh eyes, once you've explained all that. But if, in spite of all, he tries to assert my madness, I insist – note that I say insist, from the verb to insist – you're even stronger in your attitude. I authorize you to cross your arms and to adopt the air of those who demand, rather than give explanations. "I admit," – you can say to him – "that my master deeply disappointed you twenty years ago. He also disappointed all those who trusted him in one way or another. But bear in mind it was a two-way game. Because if my master disappointed all of you, you disappointed him. We were living in a world of reciprocal deception. In any case, wasn't it the Marquis who renounced your century's pageantry? Wasn't it he who shut himself up in his castle, turning his back on so much hypocrisy and selfishness? Didn't he impose upon himself a penance of twenty years' solitude? It's very wrong, therefore my Lord, to jump to hasty conclusions. Don't let's be too superficial. It seems to me that, instead of dismissing his letter with a pitying smile, you should have appreciated what this letter means. You might think that an epistle written with the earnest intention of its not being understood is an absurd epistle. But let's go a little deeper. Set on sending an illegible letter, my master could have sent it to any gentleman in the district. However, it was sent to you, precisely. And he wrote his name on the envelope as clearly as possible, so that there could be no doubt about the sender's identity. Doesn't it seem significant to you that, having decided to make a postal return to his century, he should think of you before anyone else? Isn't that a touching detail? Don't you feel honoured, finding yourself the recipient of a desperate letter? Imagine you've been shipwrecked, but able to swim to a small island. The years roll by. Not a ship on the horizon. In the bitter solitude, you learn the difficult love for palm-trees and the insects which chirp in the undergrowth. Your soul purges itself. One morning at last, you notice the outline of a rescuing sail in the distance. You immediately feel all the emotion of reunion with a world you believed lost for ever. Distraught, you rush towards the boat which comes to rescue you. Tell me, my Lord, how would you act in the circumstances? Wouldn't you leave all social refinements and restraints on one side? Would you criticize someone for the long cry which, surely, would well up in his throat? Therefore, my illustrious Lord, I think you ought to answer my master with another desperate letter this very day. You and all those who, like you, receive a missive similar to the one I've just delivered. In this way, despair would be changed into something daily, into a dazzling postal exchange. Why go on with half measures. Down with pretence, Don Demetrio. Down with pious formulas. Long live the shout, the howl, the brutal accumulation of consonants. Let's unequivocally externalize our anguish. Let's do it until we're finally able to understand the enormity of our unhappiness. Don't you, my Lord, believe that the first letter of a brilliant new alphabet might not spring from just such an absurd correspondence? Don't you think that men, frightened by so much inarticulate screaming, might not end up joining hands? Doesn't it seem that an indisputable esperanto will begin to impose itself, letting us all communicate without any more dictionaries? What I'm trying to tell you with all this, my

eminent Lord, is that we must know the nature and magnitude of our illness before deciding on medicine and
dosage. To be fully conscious of how ill we are. To
renounce once and for all ineffectual poultices. Why,
then, go on prolonging this agony?" Forgive my vehe-
mence, Bautista, I'm seeing myself in your place, handing
my own letter over to Don Demetrio and trying to convince him that, in spite of everything, God is good and
has not completely shut off all roads to our salvation.
Oh no! Don't worry, my friend! I don't want to deprive
you of the honour! It'll be you who carries the letter! I
can assure you that, if you repeat the whole of the speech
I've just suggested, Don Demetrio will start shrinking,
little by little, and will end up spiritually kneeling before
you. He may even go as far as to kiss your hands, because
we can never foresee how a man may act when he suddenly discovers that he's not alone and that there is
someone else who thinks like him. There is a problem,
however: Don Demetrio may presume to think he isn't
alone. In that case, Bautista, he'll be impervious to all
our arguments. "Why are you talking to me about
despair?" he'll ask, arching his eyebrows. "I lack for
nothing in this world," he'll explain. "My health's excellent, I'm enormously rich and I'm lucky enough to share
a bed with the most loving and affectionate wife in the
world. Can't that be called happiness?" Oh, Bautista! If
Don Demetrio has the cheek to say something similar,
I authorize you to make a show of crossing yourself, like
a pious old woman when she hears the devil mentioned.
"Happy, you?" – you then say, hoarsely. "You, who with
your six stone have spent your whole life chasing fat
maternal women capable of restoring your lost childhood's freedom from responsibility? You, who constantly proclaim your obsessive devotion to the colour
green, as if there were no other colours in the world?

You, who boast of getting by on half a dozen olives a day? Can a man who's had a diet like that for years be called happy? Doesn't that proverbial lack of appetite perhaps indicate some hidden disorder in your digestive system, perhaps some cruel cancer which may suddenly carry you off to your grave? Ah no, my good Lord! Forgive me for speaking so openly, but you're not happy, however much you'd like to be so!" At this point, cross your arms and regard Don Demetrio severely. Don't say anything for some little while, allowing him time to reflect, and you'll see the poor man break into tears. "You're right," he'll recognize – "I'm not happy. I've never been happy. It was presumptious of me to say I was." From that moment, Bautista, you can drop your intransigent attitude. Accept his excuses and try to comfort him. Forget what I said earlier about the voluptuousness of tears. Give him a hug. "Congratulations, my Lord," say to him. "Congratulations, because you've just recovered your self-awareness. You've at last noticed that you're not happy and that the world around you is a frivolous dance. But open your eyes to that other admirable world you've been ignoring up to now. I'm referring to the insect world, which moves with the order and precision of a planetary system. Insects show us the way to happiness. Did you know, my Lord, that these small creatures have given my master the most indescribable emotions? Ah yes, Don Demetrio! You too could turn to these minuscule forms of life. Draw close to these logically consistent creatures! Appraise the multiplicity of their forms and fathom the intricate labyrinth of their instincts! Praise the sincerity of their behaviour! I can assure you that after your noviciate in this world of subtle vibrations, you'll be much nearer the truth." Let's now imagine that Don Demetrio, a bit ashamed of his tears, tries to object. "You talk to me about insects' order and

sincerity," – he replies, drying his eyes with his handkerchief – "but what about their cruelty?" If the Count asks
you that question, mention the praying mantis, considered to be one of the cruellest of insects. Admit that,
yes, the praying mantis is a creature with fairly equivocal
behaviour and an insatiable appetite, pulling it towards
cannibalism. But don't accept that anyone could call it
cruel or hypocritical. The mantis always has its front feet
joined in an attitude of entreaty or prayer, but it's not
trying to deceive anybody. All it's doing is adopting the
most efficient posture. Cruelty and hypocrisy are charac-
teristics of man. But there are other insects which can't
even be unjustly accused. Without looking further,
there's the Goliath beetle. A little animal with a frightful
aspect. It doesn't have the impressive horns of the
rhinoceros beetle, but its corporeal mass is even greater.
When it unfolds its leathery black wings, their span
exceeds that of several sparrows. As you can see, a big
powerful creature, but it sometimes lets itself be captured
by charming black children and, tied to the piece of string
they carry, it meekly flies in a circle, like a purring country
merry-go-round. Tell me, Bautista, – or, rather, "tell me,
my Lord," if it's you putting this example to Don Demetrio – what man in this country would allow himself to
be captured by a swarm of Zulu children? What man
would agree to be tied by an ankle or a leg and to fly
round and round those little ebony devils? Well there
you are, Bautista, you won't be short of arguments to
convince the Count. Here he is, then, with his chin sunk
in his chest, his brow furrowed, admitting your good
sense. Perfect. Let's picture a happy end. "All right," he
says, after a deep sigh. "Given that the world has fallen
into deceit and disloyalty, I'll also escape to where its
falsity can't reach me. I'll do what your master did,
twenty years ago. In spite of everything, he was always

a clever man." At that point, my friend, we can consider your mission fulfilled. The seed will've been planted. You'll be able to ask Don Demetrio leave to withdraw and to return here with news of my victory. More likely, however, the Count won't yet let you leave his castle. "No, don't go yet, my good man," he'll say, in this case. "Stay with me until I've written my reply to the Marquis. Without more delay, I'm going to write your master a letter as absurd as the one he's just sent me. From today, he'll know he's no longer alone." Nothing more. Happy curtain. Deafening round of applause. We shan't go on torturing ourselves, shan't imagine less happy solutions. Tomorrow I'll return to writing other mad letters and the world will finally end up understanding that grief is general, and that is must adopt more urgent measures than simple Constitutional Reform. Part of this success will be yours, Bautista. So, get ready to leave for Don Demetrio's castle, and may God not take you before you've confessed. Capture the pair of frogs, dress up in green, get an umbrella – rain or shine – then come to see me, and I'll give you some fresh instructions. You must be aware that everything can't be reduced to the reception the Count may accord you. We have other enemies. People neither you nor I know, but who will in no way allow the delivery of a letter that may mean the beginning of a new Golden Age. What's wrong with you now, Bautista? Why are you making that face? Did you think all our problems were centred on Don Demetrio? I'm afraid not, my poor friend. You'll have to over- come other obstacles. It's two hours from here to Don Demetrio's castle, going at a good pace. I told you earlier you could choose between two ways, either crossing the river by the stone bridge, or going through the poplars. I asked you to take the latter because it passes through the centre of the village and I thought it would be useful if everyone saw you with my letter in your hand. But the bad thing is that when you reach the wood, those enemies I referred to can easily ambush you, hidden behind the trees. You must face this risk boldly. You're asking who these enemies are? Don't be ingenuous, for God's sake. The old enemies. All those flies who've been living off the corpse of our unhappiness and loneliness all these years. Those who enjoy, as the poet says, filtering poison into men's blood. Where are they? I'll tell you straight: they're everywhere. Just as it's rumoured. In every corner, including the most unexpected. They make up a vast organization surrounding us. They besiege our castles day and night and don't allow the most trivial *billet-doux* to enter or leave. Here's another reason, as if I hadn't enough already, to justify my letter's impenetrability. Suppose, for example, you fall into the hands of these cruel people after you've left this castle. They'll search your pockets and find the letter. Taking that possibility into account, how could I risk sending an epistle in which my wishes could be effortlessly and painlessly interpreted, as easily as an adolescent's verses, in fact? Don't you think it's more logical to resort to hieroglyphics? Isn't it better to baffle this rabble with a coded letter, in which all my immense love is masked by apparent madness? Dangers begin, then, Bautista, as soon as you're outside the castle gate. From here to Don Demetrio's is a good four or five miles. For a man who has one leg shorter than the other – or, if you prefer, one leg longer than the other – it's not going to be easy to cover that distance. You could've done the journey on horseback but, as you well know, my only horse – nostalgic for horizons – died of boredom some years back. Anyway, it's not going to be a simple stroll. The journey, I repeat, may take you more than two hours. So, if you start off at three, you could be at the Count's castle by five. But how do you feel if I now try to alert you to the risks you run on this journey? To work, then, we'll begin at the beginning. It's three o'clock in the afternoon. You're dressed in green, frogs in your pocket and an umbrella hanging from your left forearm. You're burning to go. You receive my blessing – you should know that I'm prepared to give you my blessing – and get ready to leave. The dangers begin. First of all, you mustn't leave the castle just anyhow, exposing yourself to surprise attack as soon as you've crossed the drawbridge. First, you must spy out the terrain. Climb the watchtower – or, better still, the keep – and scrutinize the landscape. Make sure there's nobody camped within a two thousand yard radius. Descend to the courtyard and, following the sentry walk, climb the flanking tower. Once up there, pay special attention to the poplar grove, which is where those swine could be waiting in ambush. Then go through the angle tower, under the portcullis, along the battlements, round the barbican surreptitiously and, finally leave through the stockade gate. What will you find, once you've left the shadow of our walls? A beautiful road which, if they're no complications, should take you to the village. A way through splendid vineyards, which seems designed for idyllic country outings. But let's look more closely at this road, don't let's be taken in by appearances. Its first mile or so crosses an unobstructed zone. During this stage, it'll be easy for you to see if a stranger is approaching, because anyone doing so must do it openly and you'll have time to put yourself on guard. So, if someone approaches, don't show alarm. On the contrary, adopt the attitude of those who have nothing to fear, of those who don't even suspect they could be victims of aggression. You could even begin to sing at the top of your voice. Then, when this potential enemy – as things stand, all strangers are potential enemies – when this potential enemy, I repeat, comes alongside you, halt, stop singing, cross your arms and look him straight in the eye without blinking. Don't be the first to speak. Wait for the other to do so. Don't forget that, after all, you're still on your lord's land and this gives you a certain authority. Let's imagine, then, that this grim character, after greeting you with an ambiguous good afternoon – which doesn't mean anything – looks up at the sky and says the clouds threaten rain. In that case, you know what to expect. "You're regrettably wasting your time," you can say. "Understand, my friend, that I'm not carrying a letter and, even if I were, you wouldn't manage to wrest it from me." Hearing this, the wayfarer will shrug his shoulders, perhaps, and raise his eyebrows, as if he didn't know what you're talking about. But don't let him take you in, because these people are expert in deception. Insist that you're not carrying any message and, while doing so, meaningfully stroke the handle of your umbrella. If you show yourself confident of your own strength, the stranger, after babbling some excuse, will make a half turn and slink off with his tail between his legs. I don't mean by that he'll definitively give up his attack, more likely he'll wait for a more favourable occasion. Until you're in that poplar grove, for example. I said a moment ago that was the most dangerous part of the journey. Five hundred yards in which you run the danger that someone, suddenly appearing from between two trees, unexpectedly blocks your way. It's not a thick wood, but it's sufficiently so to allow an ambush. They could catch you by the throat before you've time to see your aggressor's face. So be very careful and, when you get to the boundary, double your precautions. Don't move a step without first making sure. Control your breathing and sharpen your hearing. However, don't be frightened by every sound, woods are full of noises.

Neither you nor anyone can stop the insects, those admirable brothers of ours, who go on stirring their antennae and unfolding their lacy wings in wind or sun. They are not to blame for our frustrations. Remember, too, that sometimes a simple leaf, becoming detached from its branch, is enough to make a coward's heart leap. There are also animals living in the wood, and we can't deny them their right to move just because men want to cross it in silence. Birds sing, snakes crawl and rabbits make the fallen leaves rustle. That's how it's been, and that's how it always will be. Can we lay down, even by royal decree, that these creatures should give up their habitual activities? Your only remedy is to try to differentiate between noises that are suspicious and those that are not. It's quite clear, for example, that if you hear a guffaw, you should double your precautions because, apart from hyenas, the animal capable of laughter still hasn't been born. Laughter, Bautista, is something exclusive to man, so as soon as you hear it, stop and try to discover its source. Get down on the ground and crawl towards it. Make use of your elbows and move forward an inch at a time. It may be that the laughter comes from our enemies, guilty of the stupidity of celebrating our defeat in advance. But it could also be innocent woodcutters laughing. Look for an ideal observation point and calmly inspect the intruder, or better said, the intruders, because nobody laughs when he's on his own. Use all five senses in this operation. Woodcutters round here are easily identifiable. They're hefty, bearded and, from wielding axes, they have powerfully developed arms. They have check shirts and usually wear a black beret pulled down over the eyebrows. But – I'm following my custom of not overlooking any danger – there's the risk that our enemies, to allay suspicion, may disguise themselves as woodcutters, and I'm therefore advising you to note not only how they dress, but also how they look. The relationship between the soma and the psyche is nothing new. A depraved soul always has a depraved face, and vice versa. It's true that some blackguards, by dint of spending a long time in front of the mirror and resorting to very sophisticated make-up, manage to hide their real designs beneath a kindly expression, but can they also disguise those handle-like ears, so characteristic of the most dangerous criminals? Can they disguise that protuberant lower jaw, which distinguishes the worst delinquents? Can they make the occipital cavity – exclusive to big apes – disappear? Observe them very carefully, the men you discover in the clearing of the wood. Don't rush to a decision which you might later regret. You must only relax when you're convinced they are, in fact, woodcutters. But don't divulge your journey's real reason even so. Don't be rash, because good and evil frequently travel together. Nobody can be called completely honest, or utterly despicable. Men aren't like piano keys, black or white. I'm telling you all this because, learning you're bearing an important letter for the Count, one of these woodcutters, with an eye on promotion, may let the cat out of the bag. So if one of these men asks you where you're going, you must shrug your shoulders. "It's my day off," you can say. "I left my master's castle with nowhere special in mind. Perhaps I'll follow the route I'm now on and continue along this road towards the North, but maybe I'll go South, East, or West. Who knows. Freedom, my worthy woodcutters, is precisely that: when we can do anything, not knowing what to do." When you've got to this point in your speech, pause and sigh. Then add, nodding your head: "That's how it is, my rustic friends. More than a right, freedom is an obligation; it entails annoying responsibilities. Therefore I'd feel most happy if someone could now tell me what I should do and which direction I should take." It's most likely that the woodcutters, not being very bright, won't understand what you're saying. But don't be too sure about that, because more than once it's happened that peasants have mysteriously intuited the deeper meaning of their masters' lucubrations. There've even been some who got excited about the craziest enterprises. So if you're forced to give a more specific reply, make up something that won't compromise us. Cleverly modify the truth. Agree that you did leave my castle to deliver a message, but tell them that the recipient is the Duke of W, for example, not Count Demetrio. "What?" – the sharpest of the woodcutters may become distrustful – "Isn't the Duke of W's castle towards the West?" Don't lose your head, Bautista. "You're right," you reply. "The Duke of W's castle is on our left. And anyone seeing me now on this road might think I was going towards the castle of Count Don Demetrio, a gentleman my master has no interest in. But when – after going through the village – I get up to the cemetery, I'll go down the road with the cypresses, which'll take me to my proper destination." After saying all this, it might be helpful to round things off with some proverb or saying. That'll show these men that you belong to the same social class. As an afterthought, say, for example: "As you know, it's a long lane that has no turning!", or "As you know, all's well that end's well!" All these expressions, of course, refer to the long round-about way to the Duke of W's castle. I'm suggesting recourse to proverbs, Bautista, because I'm convinced that you'll gain these people's confidence more easily by displaying a certain amount of plebeian erudition. I mean, it'll take less trouble to convince them if, in spite of first appearances, they can think you and they belong to the same tribe. Once convinced, they'll firmly believe everything you say. They'll stop being suspicious. "Why shouldn't we believe what this comrade says?" they'd reply to anyone questioning their explanations. "What interest could he have in lying? Isn't he too under a landowner's boot?" So win these men's confidence. By the thread you'll know the reel: I don't want them to start investigating, once you've gone. A little demagogy never goes amiss, though they say out there that demagogy is the hypocrisy of power. Fire off all the proverbs you can remember, whether or not to the point. "My friends," – you can say, as you're setting off – "a rolling stone gathers no moss." (There's one for you.) "I mean, I'd like to say with you till nightfall, but duty first and foremost" (There's a second.) "It's now time for me to go on my way to the Duke of W's castle, because it's the early bird that catches the worm." (A third.) If you fire off all this advice naturally, you'll leave the woodcutters as firm friends, prepared to swear that the Duke of W is the one and only recipient of my letter. They'll move aside and let you leave. I can see them waving their berets in the air in goodbye. It would be a beautiful ending. On the other hand, imagine that these woodcutters are no such thing, imagine they're fearsome criminals hired by our enemies. While waiting for you in the clearing, they were sharpening their knives on a stone. They come to meet you, they surround you, they draw their swords. "All right, let's have that letter, or I'll slit your throat," the gang's leader threatens. He's not talking for the fun of it, he's quite prepared to kill you. You wouldn't be his first victim: such men are born violent, they live violently and always find good reasons for killing their fellow men. Don't start trembling again, Bautista, and think for a moment. What could you do in this situation? I'll tell you straight away: forget about heroic acts and hand over the letter. But do so with a long justification. "Very well, gentlemen," – say to them – "here's my master's letter. I don't understand a single word of it, and I'm not prepared to risk my life for something I can't understand. You should know – and now you'll be able to check for yourselves – this letter's completely incomprehensible. Before handing it to me, my master was cruel enough to read it to me from beginning to end, and I swear I was really disappointed. The same thing'll happen to you, assuming you know how to read. I think that's what's going to offend most, because letters like this are always an insult to our illiteracy and our demand for clear answers. You work it out yourselves: faced with our concrete needs, which can be replied to monosyllabically, these exquisite big shots allow themselves the luxury of abstraction. Instead of concerning themselves about our food stocks, they devote themselves to ramifying word games. Here's the letter, then, and do with it whatever you want." Let's now try to foresee what may happen after your exposition. The head bandit is mistrustful. He brusquely seizes the letter and tears the envelope open. He wants to show his men that he, at least, can read. His authority can emerge from this episode strengthened. But when he looks at the text, he discovers its hieroglyphics. He clears his throat and shoots a dignified look at his men. He tries reading again and fails. He persists and finds his good will counts for nothing. He flushes with shame but doesn't dare tell his followers that the letter's gibberish because he's frightened they won't believe him. Seeing his uncertainty, some of the desperados smile maliciously, deciding they're led by a man as ignorant as they are. The chief's authority, instead of being strengthened, is dented. What can a man do in that dangerous position, Bautista? Anything, rather than let his people sneer. He may even dump his anger on you – yes, my poor friend, on you! – rather than allow his men to mock him. Not for personal revenge – a messenger is never responsible for the message he carries – but to regain lost prestige. It wouldn't be the first time a man resorts to his sword, when his reasoning fails, would it Bautista? Isn't history full of examples? We must avoid its being your fate. Yes, we must avoid it, because you deserve something better than death at the hands of some outlaws, on account of a letter you didn't even write! Let's ward off that danger. What, my faithful friend, if you leave the castle this afternoon with two letters? I'll explain: one letter, the authentic one – the one that interests us – stuck to your solar plexus, like a piece of elastoplast, so that no one can find it. Another, the false one – which I'll write in a jiffy, while you're hunting the frogs – and which you'll bear in your hand. Both written on green paper and addressed to Don Demetrio. If you're captured, you give the bandits the false one, of course, and they'll be able to read it without any trouble. Any subject will do. A very sad letter of condolence, for example, on the death of one of the Count's relatives I had the luck not to know. Or a note assuring him that, in spite of everything, I remember him in my prayers. Perhaps a letter of congratulation on the birth of his heir, which happened twenty-four years ago. Well, anything will do, we shan't bother about that now. The important thing is that the chief of this band of highwaymen can read my handwriting. Isn't that the best solution, Bautista? To summarize: you surrender the false letter to the rogue and withdraw a couple of paces. Let him show off his intelligence and then noisily celebrate with his men the success of their mission, behind which lies the name of some great personage whose identity most likely we'll never know. While the bandits are given over to the worst excesses, you, full of remorse – as if you'd really handed over the real letter – continue to withdraw, one step at a time, but still without turning your back on them. Then, when you're far enough away, turn and begin to run at breakneck speed. Leave the wood and, when you get to the mill, take the path to the village. Now remember what I said at the beginning: go down the main street, take the first turning on the right and you reach the stone cross. The Count's castle is directly opposite. Hurry, to make up for time lost because of the highwaymen. Pay good attention to what I'm going to say next, because it's more important than all that's been said up to now: if Don Demetrio's castle no longer exists, if it was demolished twenty years ago to make way for a block of council housing, if they've turned it into a state tourist hotel, if his property has been expropriated to build a motorway, there's no need to come back to bring me the news. I'll know that I'm finally alone and that there's no remedy for my grief. And I'll stay here with my insects, those tiny palpitating lives halfway between mineral and spirit. Maybe that's my fate. Perhaps, my dear unselfish Bautista, the time has come for me to accept that *les jeux sont faits*, as they say in Monte Carlo.'

DEAR MONSTER

DEAR MOTHER

He's sitting behind an enormous desk and doesn't even make a pretence of getting up when I come into his office. He limits himself to shaking hands. He has china-blue eyes, which match his tie, straw-coloured hair, rosy cheeks and the sharp nose of a scheming cleric. On the whole, he looks good-natured. But we'll see what happens. He invites me to sit down, smiles encouragingly and introduces himself as H.J. Krugger, the Personnel Director. He speaks with a slight foreign accent, dragging his r's and blurring his vowels. He wants to make it clear from the very beginning that the methods he uses to pick the Bank's future employees are fairly unorthodox and that our interview is going to be quite a long one. I must answer all his questions, even those that may seem extremely intimate, without omitting a single detail (including the most insignificant) because the tell-tale fact could be hidden in any one of those details. He has my file on the table, but he asks me to confirm some personal data.

My big moment has come. I tell him I'm called Juan D., that I'm now thirty years old, that I lost my father when I was still a child and that I live with a mother who idolizes me, but makes my life impossible.

Krugger briefly consults the file and asks how could it be that I didn't even finish my primary schooling. I tell him that my mother – to save me from the other children, who took pleasure in tearing up my exercise books and

jabbing me with their compasses – made me leave school
before I was eight. From then on, it was she who personally supervised my education, using the same text books
I would've had at school, but sometimes giving them a
pretty personal interpretation.

He wants to know about my last employment. An
essential question. I confess that I've never worked, and
he's astonished that there could still exist today a man
who has survived thirty years without needing to work.
I reply by telling him that if he knew my mother's obsession about having me constantly tied to her apron-strings
he wouldn't be surprised. After a fashion (I tell him) she
is to blame for my not having worked.

He's beginning to understand that my mother plays
an important role in my life. He clears his throat, raises
his eyebrows and lights a cigarette. He wants to know
what reasons prompted me to write to them. The daily
papers are full of offers of employment. Why did I choose
them precisely?

I try to reply concisely and briefly, without being long-
winded. I tell him that the first reason (and the most
important) was the over-riding need to start work, so as
not to go on living off others. Another (which explains
why I wrote to them precisely) was the profound respect
I've always had for banks, which for me are like lay
cathedrals, temples of aluminium and steel in which
men's work and savings are rewarded in this world.

He shakes his head, perhaps surprised by my meta-
phors, incongruous from a man who has hardly ever
been to school. Perhaps it's the first time he hears banks
called cathedrals. After his initial surprise, he looks me
straight in the eye, as if trying to discover whether I'm
pulling his leg. I hold his gaze without blinking, until his
suspicious expression fades. I proceed to tell him that I

wrote the letter behind my mother's back, while she was
in the kitchen, but that she found out what I had in my
hand and then got terribly angry.

Why? he asks me politely, amid the bluish clouds of
smoke emitted by his cigarette.

It's not easy to answer in a couple of words and I shrug
my shoulders. I see him smile slightly, as if accepting
and, up to a point, understanding an applicant's shyness
and inhibitions. He allows a short pause and then repeats
that he needs to know every detail of the life of those
aspiring to work in the Bank, because those details (however trivial they may seem) have a habit of growing and
later affecting the daily round, with all that that implies
for the good management of any enterprise. He adds that
nobody can distinguish the small from the big without
running the risk of being mistaken, and that it is precisely
the little details that can best reveal a man's real character.

I have no alternative, then, but to go into details, however
distressing that may be. I breathe in deeply through my
nose, adjust myself in the armchair and tell him that my
mother can't bear the idea of being at home alone, not
even for a few hours, because she needs me continuously
at her side. Starting from this premiss (I add), you can
well imagine my problems.

He blinks and flicks ash from his cigarette into the
ashtray. For a moment, his expression becomes tenser,
as if he's beginning to discover in my candidature some
peculiar circumstance, the correct interpretation and
handling of which will call for some special effort on his
part. He asks me to recount what happened then, after
my mother had found out about the letter.

Well (I tell him), when she learnt that I was applying
for a job as a night watchman, she was overcome by

laughter. Then, when her spring had run down, she gave me a tremendous ticking off. She was about to tear up the letter, but I got it out of her hands before she could do so. I put the sheet of paper in an envelope, ran out of the house and posted the letter in a pillar box. When I got back home, I found my mother collapsed in an easy chair, gasping like a fish out of water.

Krugger again shakes ash from his cigarette. He's silent for a moment, weighing up what I've just told him. Then he purses his lips and, carefully measuring his words, says that my mother's attitude seems more or less normal to him and that she's not the first mother who's unable to live for long without her children (especially an only child). He gives me a sideways glance and waits for me to reply or, at least, to raise some objection. His game is obvious: he wants to draw me out and to drag me into a full and compromising confession in which I blacken my mother. However, I'm sensible and I keep quiet. When he understands that he's not going to get anywhere along that track, he attacks on another flank: he refers, as if incidentally, to the remorse that must have assailed me when, home again, I found my mother half-fainting in her armchair.

Smiling, I tell him that it hadn't worried me to find her in such a state, because my mother is an accomplished actress and I realized immediately that she was putting on one of her performances. So I didn't allow myself to be affected (I add). I sat in my chair, opposite her, and I reminded her that I was now thirty years old and wasn't prepared to lose the chance of working in a bank, even in the humblest of occupations.

Krugger frowns. He doesn't agree with what I've just said and he makes no attempt to disguise his disagreement. He's of the opinion that to work as a night watchman

in a bank (above all, in his bank) is not a humble occu-
pation, but the very opposite. He thinks, in fact, that to
guard the wealth of others, in return for a limited wage,
demands a high spirit of sacrifice from those who are
guarding it, and an altruism worthy of praise. He stubs
out his cigarette in the ashtray and in the silence which
follows I can, for the first time, hear the wheezing of his
lungs. I don't, now, know what to say and I limit myself
to watching the sunbeam which is filtering through the
window and falling directly on the top of his desk.

To risk our life for money that doesn't belong to us
(he insists) is a genuine way of becoming a saint.

I realize that I must quickly rectify my mistake. Actually (I say to him), that's what I think, too. And it's more
or less what I said to my mother. But she didn't give way.
From the depths of her chair, she advised me to give up
silly escapades, because the two of us could get by perfectly well with her widow's pension. She also said that
only the poor worked and that, thanks be to God, we
were far from being so. Hearing this, I couldn't help smiling, remembering the dire straits we're in at the end of
each month. Then she saw the feebleness of her argument and began to talk about the great dangers which
lie in wait for children of good families these days, outside in the street.

Krugger raises his forefinger. He wants to know if my
mother, in using the word 'street', was making a general
reference to everything beyond the confines of our home.
I reply, yes indeed, she used that word in its widest sense,
and that it wasn't the first time she'd used it thus, because
for her the world has always been divided into two parts,
one which falls within the confines of our home and one
which lies without.

So, little by little, we're getting deeply involved. Krugger lights another cigarette and is absorbed by the smoke circling up to the ceiling. I go on to tell him (without his needing to ask) that my mother (always looking for new arguments to make me give up) referred to the nervous tic which, since the previous day, had given her left eyelid no peace and which, according to her, was warning her of the dangers in which I was going to find myself, if I didn't drop my work plans. Krugger listens to me without shifting his gaze from the spiral of smoke. With a faint smile, he gives his opinion that my mother is a resourceful woman and that it would never have occurred to him to think that a simple nervous tic could become a harbinger of fate. I tell him that neither do I believe in that or similar stupidities, and so I gave her to understand, but I made the mistake of making my observation with a smile, so that she wrongly interpreted my benevolent attitude.

I think (I go on to tell Krugger) that she thought she was beginning to convince me. Can you imagine, she took my hand and tried to get me to sit on her knees. I didn't accept her invitation and she had to be content with holding my hand. She then said (still referring to her tic) that God employs the most insignificant details to show us the best path to follow. And then (growing bolder because I didn't reply and talking more and more nonsense) she added that she knew very well the day unavoidably came when each little boy wanted to feel himself a man, but that day hadn't yet come for me, because she and I still had a lot of things to do together.

A nostalgic spark is ignited in Krugger's blue gaze. He comments that my mother's words seem beautiful to him and I reply saying that perhaps they could be in other circumstances, but that they didn't seem so to me at that moment and that, hearing her come out with all those absurdities, I thought it was now time to take the bull by the horns and to speak clearly.

Then (I continue) I plucked up my courage, withdrew my hand from hers and let fly that what she wanted was to have me shut up at home all my life, playing with the electric train she'd given me on my twelfth birthday.

Krugger softly snorts and stretches his legs under the table. He makes a vague gesture with the hand that is holding his cigarette and recalls that he, too, had his electric train. A little train that, by a coincidence, his mother likewise gave him on his sixth birthday. He is silent for a couple of minutes and then he evokes other beloved toys: an army of lead soldiers, a cardboard horse, a monkey with little bells. A plush monkey, of course. He also recollects a warm bedroom, a red carpet and rain gently falling on the window-panes. The wheezing of his lungs, meanwhile, is becoming more acute.

Is it usual (I ask myself) for a businessman to be so sentimental in the middle of a working day?

It's as if he'd read my thoughts. He rubs his brow, sighs and apologizes for his daydreaming. He says that he doesn't usually have time to remember his childhood but that, when he does, it's like falling into a sweet well from which it isn't easy to emerge. He sits up straight, puts on a more professional air and expresses interest in my mother's reaction after I'd blurted out all that about the train.

She adopted the attitude of an offended queen (I tell him) and began to pontificate about the conceit of children, bragging about knowing everything when in fact they know very little. She also told me that such conceit carried within it the sin of pride, for which one usually had to pay heavily later. Then, to temper her words a little, she added that the act of working, considered as such, was not in itself bad, and in circumstances different from mine it could even have a positive value, but that in my case it was a foolishness, because she was prepared to buy me a grand piano, no matter the cost, and to pay for the best music-teacher in town.

I see his expression sharpen, like a sentry who, in the middle of the night, suddenly hears the sound of distant footsteps. He takes the cigarette out of his mouth and looks me straight in the eye. He wants to know if I like music and waits for my answer expectantly.

I'm not stupid: it's clear from his attitude that he'd like me to say no, but I don't find it easy to lie and so I evade the question. I tell him that the one who likes music is my mother. He repeats the question in a more peremptory tone and I've no alternative but to confess that music makes my hair stand on end and that, at times, it seems to me politically suspect, because it suggests utopias and induces softness in people.

I think this is the reply that best fits the tastes of a night watchman and even those of a realistic, pragmatic businessman, no friend of fantasies and visions. Any other reply could work against a man who has to spend the night with his eyes wide open. Keeping watch is a task that doesn't entail heavy burdens of a cultural nature, but it demands from those who undertake it a swiftness of reflex not usually found in people who, like fanatical music-lovers, live to the strains of distant violins.

My words seem to please him, but he wants me to understand that, in spite of everything, he still keeps a little corner of his heart for the nobler feelings. He recognizes that there's a type of music which can be politically suspect, but he also admits that, at certain moments, it serves to lighten our loneliness and to sustain our hopes for a better world.

Anyway (he adds, looking at me directly) I can't imagine

you playing a Chopin sonata. You don't look like a musician.

It's possibly a trap he's laying for me to see how far my musical knowledge stretches and, indirectly, to discover if I really don't like music. If I now tell him that I adore Chopin and that, as they say, he makes me weep over my neighbour's misfortunes, he could infer that I lied earlier. I raise my eyebrow and ask him who Chopin is, but he doesn't respond. It may be that he doesn't know. Again he looks at me directly and admits that he's never been able to understand the obsession women have for imagining their sons (no matter how ugly and unpolished) changed into princes. Then he shakes his head and a melancholy smile returns to his face.

I was also predestined to study the piano (he says) but my mother died before she was able to keep me seated on a stool in front of the keyboard.

It's quite clear he's lulled by pleasant longings and it may even be that it is I who, without intending to, aroused them. He bites his lower lip (simultaneously swallowing his early memories) and wants to know what happened after my mother suggested I should study music.

I flatly refused (I tell him) and at first she seemed calmer, as if initially it consoled her to think that it wasn't going to be necessary to buy me a piano. But slowly, like a wind which is rising and ends up as a hurricane, she was getting more and more irritated. She even got to the point of insulting me, calling me an ass. More precisely, she said there are asses who think themselves deer and, when they jump, they plunge headlong.

I'm beginning to think (Krugger exclaims, regarding me with compassion) your lady mother has a certain degree of egotism.

Once again he's trying to lead me on, but I don't

swallow the bait. I loosen my tie, shift into a new position and keep quiet. Krugger now begins to address himself to the variety of situations that can exist between mothers and sons. He recalls that only a fortnight ago, in the very seat I'm now occupying, a lad of more or less my age was sitting.

That lad (he continues) had never worked either, but in contrast with you, he hadn't the slightest desire to start. I asked him if he could give me one valid justification for his attitude and he said he'd give me not just one, but a hundred thousand, the main one of which, however, was his tortoise-man nature, which obliged him to stay at home all day, just as real tortoises always remain inside theirs. He said all this quite seriously; I realized this at once, because I learnt a long time ago to recognize the smart-alecs who try to pull my leg or, at least, to disconcert me with their replies. Believe me, that lad was completely barmy. Playing along, I asked him why he thought he was a tortoise and he told me that from childhood he'd felt fascinated by those animals and that when he went to school he couldn't resist the impulse to hide his head between his shoulders and then to extend it very slowly, stretching his neck a fraction of an inch at a time, and staring hypnotically at his nearest classmate. What can you do in such cases? Nothing. Bow respectfully before the unfathomable mysteries of the human soul. I escorted that poor lad to the door, patting his back. A back which, because of its curvature and the pattern of the shirt he was wearing (I must also tell you), was like a tortoise-shell. Then, from the window, I saw him cross the street accompanied by his mother, who held him lovingly by the arm. Throughout the interview, that woman was waiting for him at the door of the Bank. She, of course, is the only heroine in the story I'm telling you. Do you understand what I'm trying to say.

Up to a point, I reply.

That lad (Krugger explains) came to see me at his mother's behest and I'm quite sure they went on from here to look for work somewhere else. Personally, I find touching that unhappy woman's obsession with trying to snatch her son from the claws of madness in order to place him in a normal world, which we may or may not like, but which we cannot disregard. Now do you understand what I'm driving at? You want to start work, but your lady mother is determined to keep you wrapped up in cottonwool, the way they once kept premature babies alive. Your mother, my dear fellow, is convinced that the sun shines only on you and that, for you, she is not only the law, but also providence and the only possible form of love.

You may be right (I cautiously admit), it may be as you say.

But I don't make the mistake of commenting on his harangue and I stay on my guard. Look out (I think), because it may be that he's invented this story to force me to compare my mother with the tortoise-boy's mother.

Krugger, it seems, is a man fond of setting traps or, at least, of getting answers through devious means. So I don't risk saying that I'd prefer to have a mother who was always pushing me out to work, and he's beginning to understand that I'm not someone he can easily manipulate. For the second time, he opens my file and checks some fact he hadn't perhaps taken into account. Without looking up from the documents, he asks me what time it was when my mother called me an ass. I tell him that it would have been more or less five o'clock on Monday afternoon, and he justifies his – apparently stupid – question by saying that his knowing this detail will help him to order my account chronologically and to put the various situations I'm recounting in their place.

Because (he explains) a situation which occurs at mid-day requires a different evaluation from a similar situation, with identical formal elements, which occurs at three in the morning.

What he's just said seems pretty trite to me, but I nod assent. Everyone's got oddities of his own. I tell him that when she called me an ass, I started to bray, as if proving her right, and that she, so as not to hear me, shut herself up in her room; I shut myself in mine, and we didn't see each other again till supper-time.

When I came back into the dining-room (I go on to say), I found her sitting at the table, with tears in her eyes, but the supper ready. It would have been already nine by then. I was surprised that, in spite of the row, she'd had sufficient energy to cook me an onion soup and a couple of fried eggs. I said I was sorry about the braying and, during supper, doing the minimum required to keep up appearances, we exchanged a few words about the upstairs neighbour, who has the habit of dragging chairs along the corridor. But we didn't discuss my plans. After a little while, she asked me to take the dirty plates to the kitchen, said goodnight and went to bed.

Krugger assents. It seems that, at last, I'm beginning to relate things as he wants to hear them. Nevertheless, he asks if he can put a bit of order into the narrative.

I seem to recall (he says, leaning back in his chair and half-closing his eyes) that you read our advertisement on Monday morning and wrote to us immediately while your lady mother was in the kitchen. She found out about the letter and got angry. You got it out of her hands before she could tear it up. You went out and posted it. On your return, you both went on arguing until five in the afternoon. Round abut then, she called you an ass and you began braying. You both shut yourselves up in your rooms and met again for supper. Perfect. You exchanged a few words about a neighbour (a kind of tacit accord to evade the matter dividing you and so to avoid further argument), and you both went to bed. We've now covered the first day of hostilities (if you'll allow me to put it like that). But from Monday till today, we're left with four days: Tuesday, Wednesday, Thursday and practically all of the morning of today, Friday. What happened during those four days? Did you go on arguing? Did you come to blows? Or, on the contrary, did you sign a peace treaty?

Let's take it stage by stage (I suggest), because there's still a lot to relate. Monday night (in other words, at the end of our first day of hostilities, as you put it) I went to bed convinced that my mother would adopt a more reasonable attitude the following day. However, it was an effort to get to sleep and I stayed awake for a couple of hours. You'll appreciate that, after spending a day arguing, I felt somewhat overwrought. She too had trouble getting to sleep: I heard her gently sobbing for some time. In the end she was silent and I again felt optimistic. Tomorrow she'll be as soft as silk, I thought. But I was completely wrong because she spent the next two days (Tuesday and Wednesday) without saying a word to me, though she did go on performing her housekeeper role. Believe me, it wasn't easy to put up with that silence and I spent the whole of Tuesday singing between my teeth. A strategy for weaning her from her silence came to me on Wednesday morning. My mother's an excellent cook and she's always been very proud of her culinary skills. I thought that if I cast doubt on these skills, I'd manage to unhinge her and, ultimately, oblige her to speak. She won't put up with my criticism in silence, I thought. So I attacked her *paella*. I said it was inedible, that you could find better *paellas* in the port's meanest, cheapest restaurant. That was at lunch. At supper, I pretended to spit in the soup. But on neither occasion did I succeed in dragging a word out of her. Nothing I said seemed to matter to her. She confined herself to listening to me impassively and to eating in silence. I left the soup in the plate and went off to bed without giving her a kiss on the forehead and without wishing her goodnight. That was like a blow to her. Then, while I was undressing, I began to sing at the top of my lungs, hoping that she'd make me shut up, but she didn't and I heard her slaving away in the kitchen for quite a long time.

2

Krugger is now listening to me without moving a muscle of his face. He wants to know when exactly my mother spoke to me again.

It was on Thursday morning (I tell him), yesterday, that is. The postman brought me your letter at about eleven. I sat down in my chair, I unfolded the letter with an air of triumph and read it silently, but ostensibly moving my lips, as if savouring that first victory. I mean, I didn't worry about hiding my joy. My mother, who was sitting in her armchair knitting, watched me uneasily for a few minutes. She couldn't keep quiet any longer and she asked me: Who's your letter from? I deliberately repeated her question a couple of times. The Bank, I finally answered. What do they say? was her next question, her voice trembling slightly. They want to interview me and they've fixed an appointment for tomorrow, I replied with a smile. She was going to say something else, but she restrained herself. She went back to her knitting and didn't speak to me again throughout the morning. However, when it was lunch-time, she gave me a plate of macaroni with tomato sauce, knowing full well that I prefer it *au gratin* and that I can't stand tomatoes. Perhaps you're thinking it's a triviality, but I, who know her very well, am sure it was her way of letting me know that my gastronomic preferences would no longer be taken into account and that she wasn't going to worry about satisfying my whims.

I concur, murmurs Krugger.

Her revenge (I continue) seemed so childish to me that I was moved more to tenderness than to anger. What would you have done in my place? Make a fuss? I decided more is achieved by sweetness than by bitterness, so I put the plate of macaroni on one side, looked at her patiently and said it was time for us to begin acting sensibly and not like little children. I reminded her that the umbilical cord which once joined us together, had been severed a long time since, that time flew and that, however much she regretted it, I'd become a fully-fledged man.

You certainly expressed yourself clearly, Krugger allows.

But it was no use (I tell him) because she, as always, got hold of the wrong end of the stick. She asked me what I meant her to understand by saying that time flew and that I'd become a fully-fledged man. I suppose, she added, it's a way of telling me I'm old. I didn't lose my composure (you'll appreciate I had reasons enough to do so) and I stated precisely that it wasn't that she'd grown old, but that, unavoidably, I'd stopped being young. This reply didn't satisfy her and she stuck to her suspicions. She said that whatever I might think, mothers (herself, for example) never grow old, at least in relation to their own children, which was the same as admitting that the sway they have over the fruit of their womb is a right which belongs to them for life, that is, a right which isn't subject to prescriptions, in the same way that a child's obligations to its mother cannot be prescribed. Do you see her way of tangling up words?

During these last few minutes, the sky has become increasingly covered by clouds. Krugger gets up and goes over to the window, as if worried by the possibility of rain. But it isn't rain that's worrying him. Without turning round, he tells me that I'm putting him in a dilemma: on the one hand, he can't fail to appreciate the worth of my firm decision to start work; on the other, he feels profoundly moved by my mother's attitude.

You'll point out (he adds, keeping a watch on me through the window panes) that this Personnel Department should be guided by more professional criteria and independently of subjective considerations. That would be most logical and what this Bank's Board of Directors expects of me. But in spite of all that, I can't help taking into account the suffering of that excellent woman. The love she feels for you borders on the irrational, perhaps, but, when it's sincere, isn't love always irrational?

I've the impression that, telling me all this, he's exaggerating his foreign accent. I don't know how to reply. He moves away from the window, sits down again, is quiet for a moment, and then, adopting a more casual air, he says that, without knowing exactly why, he has the impression that my mother must be a woman with an aristocratic demeanour, with very fair hair gathered in a bun, eyes slightly separated from the base of the nose and a blue gaze seeming to come from on high.

Nothing like (I tell him), you're completely wrong. My mother's eyes and hair are black, and, to make herself look younger, she's got a permanent wave.

I could also tell him that she must weigh around fifteen stone, but I think that would be getting too detailed. Krugger lights another cigarette and smiles a bit disappointedly. It's possible that, in describing my mother, he'd sketched a portrait of his own, as he imagines her in his dreams. He closely examines the tip of his cigarette, clicks his tongue and, once again guessing my thoughts, accuses himself of being an incorrigible sentimentalist. He allows a few minutes to pass in silence, re-orders his ideas and tries to recover his role as interviewer. He asks me to go on with my story from the moment she spoke about a child's obligations.

Try to picture the scene (I say): she and I seated on either side of the table, separated by a bottle of wine and, more significantly, by a dish of macaroni in tomato sauce. After she'd uttered her tirade, she lowered her eyes to her plate and began to eat in silence. She didn't want to see me still sitting there with my arms crossed and not touching the macaroni. I was briefly tempted to get up from the table, but I managed to overcome the temptation and I sat there watching while she, having finished her macaroni, also ate mine and, glass by glass, liquidated the bottle of wine. When she got up to take the dirty plates to the kitchen, I didn't offer to help her, as I usually do. I went to sit in my armchair and buried myself in a magazine, to show her that, even on an empty stomach, I was getting more and more interested in what went on in the world. After half an hour (it would've then been round about four), she came back into the dining-room, drying her hands on her apron. She sat in her armchair and started smiling mysteriously, as if reflecting on some idea that had occurred to her while she was doing the dishes. I put the magazine to one side and got ready to stand up to her, because my mother, when she smiles to herself, is (ignoring the differences) like the bull who bellows before it charges.

Krugger interrupts me. He wants to know why I'm always so careful to distinguish between 'her' armchair and 'my' armchair, as if she couldn't sit in mine, or I in hers. I explain to him that, in effect, she has her chair and I have mine, that neither can sit in the other's chair, and that it's like a tacit agreement which we've scrupulously observed for many years.

The fact is (I continue, ignoring his perplexed look) that she was adopting an increasingly sibylline air, as if the six or seven glasses (added to those she'd very possibly drunk while she was in the kitchen) had given her some new, irrefutable arguments. Finally, she showed her hand. She asked me the time of my interview with you today. When I told her you'd summoned me for two o'clock, she shrugged her shoulders, as if my reply had partly relieved her anxieties. She said that I still had twenty hours to think better of it. I retorted that I'd thought things out carefully and that those twenty hours were there to kill as far as I was concerned. Then she looked at me as if I'd just blasphemed. She said there was no such thing as time to kill and begged me once again to take things calmly, to be patient, and not to jump into things, because there was no appointment that could not be postponed. What do you think of her cunning: she wasn't any longer asking me not to attend this interview, but saying think again before it's too late.

Krugger shakes his head several times, assessing my mother's manoeuvre.

As you can imagine (I proceed), I was intransigent. I told her that you'd summoned me for two o'clock and that I wasn't thinking of keeping you waiting for a single minute. She didn't consider herself defeated. She looked at me brightly and said that she'd just had a wonderful idea. Do you know what it was?

How could I, murmurs Krugger.

She suggested (I tell him) I arrive for the interview twenty-four hours late, in other words, tomorrow at the same time, and if you were to draw it to my attention, I, dismayed, should say I'd mistaken the day.

Krugger sighs deeply while the first drops of rain, falling aslant, begin to hit the window panes. It's his opinion that mother's no fool, because he, too, finds it more excusable to be twenty-four hours late than ten or twelve minutes.

That's what she thought (I go on to tell him), that you would accept my apologies and not attach too much importance to my mistake, because bankers (that is, people who work in banks) are used to dealing with every type of rascal. She also pointed out that my ruse (in the event of your discovering it) might even amuse you, because in these days craftiness and cunning are more highly regarded than intelligence. As you can imagine, I didn't take her seriously. Her suggestion seemed to me so stupid that I decided it didn't deserve a reply. So I kept quiet and she made another mistake. She wrongly interpreted my silence, thinking it meant consent. She went to the kitchen, came back with another bottle of wine and, while she was uncorking it, she guiltily admitted she'd put tomatoes in the macaroni only to annoy me, but that she was now ready to cook something I liked.

Terrific (Krugger exclaims, smiling). Why didn't you take the opportunity to ask for a stuffed pheasant?

She was in an embarrassing position (I responded), but at that moment I wasn't in the mood for jokes. I refused her offer, but she insisted and said that I had to eat something, because growing boys can't go all day on an empty stomach. I answered that no man of thirty was still growing and she let out a loud laugh, as if she'd just heard a joke. Who told you you were thirty? she exclaimed. I was dumbfounded, not knowing what to reply and beginning to wonder whether she was going mad. In the end, by dint of insisting, she got me to accept a couple of fried eggs. She cooked them for me in the twinkling of an eye, with the dispatch of a landlady who's trying to regain the favour of a guest who wants to change lodgings. Then she tried to amuse me by recounting some of the latest local gossip. She talked about the door-keeper's limp (she woke up a fortnight ago with one leg paralysed), about the widow upstairs (the one who drags chairs along the corridor), and about the boyfriend of the baker's daughter, who had given himself a bump with his motorbike a couple of days previously. Little occurrences restricted to within a radius of five hundred yards of our house, you must realize. The worst of it is, all the time she was telling me this, she was drinking like a fish. She wanted me to accompany her, but I flatly refused. I turned my glass upside down and, not noticing, she poured wine all over the tablecloth. Trying to rescue the tablecloth, she poured salt on the stain and, to ease the tension, I now tried to crack an easy joke; I said that she was trying to get me drunk so she could then have me sign a document in which I promised never to work. It was a mistake, because that joke reminded her that I was standing firm and that she wasn't going to get me to give up my plans and convictions.

What did she do then? Krugger inquires.

She poured herself another glass of wine (I reply) and drank it straight down, as if it were medicine. She snorted and after a moment's silence (during which the effects of alcohol seemed to evaporate), she got back to the same old rigmarole. She again said what a grave sin it was for a son to spend his days away from home, abandoning a poor widowed mother to the bitterest sort of loneliness. She also repeated that I didn't need to work and that I could do without the half dozen cents which, at the most, you'd be able to pay me.

Krugger smiles, but decides it's not the right moment to interrupt me. His expression is now that of a man who's listening to an amusing story.

To finish off that fresh salvo (I go on to explain to him) she notified me that badly paid jobs end up demoralizing people and that, if I agreed to work for you for a pittance, I'd run the risk of becoming a frustrated youth. She also said that this frustration could harm our relationship, which hitherto (apart from an occasional squabble) had always been excellent.

Krugger looks me straight in the eye, taken by some idea which has suddenly occurred to him. He wants to know if I'm fond of reading and I tell him I'm not, that I occasionally glance at the papers or some magazine. I'm persuaded to give him this answer for the same reasons which earlier counselled me to hide my love of music. He doesn't seem convinced, but doesn't pursue the matter. He lights another of his cigarettes and wants to know what time it was when my mother gave me the fried eggs and bacon.

I didn't take the bait. I remind him that I didn't mention fried eggs and bacon, only fried eggs. I emphasize this clarification because it could well be that he is setting another of his traps to check how far I'm being faithful to the facts I'm narrating. But he's no fool either and, to justify his slip of the tongue, he comments that fried eggs are nearly always served with bacon, or with something else as garnish, fried potatoes for example. At least (he adds) my mother invariably served them with a peppery salami. And I assure you that she was an excellent cook, too.

There's something here that doesn't quite fit. Before, he said that his mother died when he was still a child. Now he confesses that she was an excellent cook and that she prepared fried eggs with peppery salami. I ask myself: is it usual for children of six or eight to eat peppery salami from their own mothers' hands? One's faced with a matter that deserves some explanation, no doubt about it, but it doesn't seem to me the right moment to express my surprise. I don't hint at my suspicion (actually, I don't know what I should suspect him of), and to change the subject and to lead the conversation down a different path, I gaily say that I don't believe that his mother was a better cook than mine.

That's impossible, I tell him.

Krugger solemnly shakes his head in denial, but without losing his friendly expression. He opens one of the desk's drawers and shows me a little red-covered notebook.

Look at this (he exclaims, flourishing the notebook as if it were a flag), I don't intend to start an argument, but this notebook could demonstrate to any knowledgeable person that my mother was an exceptional cook. Better than yours? Worse? It's not easy to begin an argument about something that definitely can't now be proved, but earlier you gave me to understand that your mother only knew how to do macaroni *au gratin* or with tomato sauce. Here, in this little book (in which my mother used to note down all her recipes) you'll find at least half a dozen different dishes based on macaroni.

And what does that prove? I ask him, keeping on with the joke.

It shows (he responds) that my mother's repertory, at least, was much wider than your mother's.

He opens the little book at the page marked M, chooses a recipe at random, and one by one enumerates all the ingredients of a macaroni salad: egg, Bologna sausage, frozen peas, onion, parsley, gherkins in vinegar, oil and, of course, macaroni. Then he closes the book and presses it gently against his breast in an ecstasy of tenderness which seems to me excessively theatrical. He says he found this book at the bottom of an old trunk a couple of years ago and that it was like finding a letter from a beloved, long since disappeared.

In a certain way (he murmurs) it's as if my mother were at my side through her handwriting, with her unusual and inimitable way of doing capitals and the very light stroke of every letter.

It's also a bit suspicious that a man who occupies a position of responsibility in the management of a business enterprise has the habit of bringing such a dearly loved, personal item to his office. Krugger has noticed my slightly surprised expression and, yet again, he guesses what I'm thinking. After sighing, he admits that whenever work permits he has recourse to the little book to reunite himself with his mother through her old culinary recipes and that doing so is as if he were inhaling a little tenderness, although it is only to be able to listen more benevolently to the (sometimes boring) confidences of the Bank's would-be employees. Then I ask him if he's also bored by me and he tells me no, that, on the contrary, with me something strange is happening.

With you (he assures me) I get the impression that I'm talking to an old friend. I identify with you through some feeling that I'm incapable of defining. Perhaps we share too many coincidences. It's why my way of conducting this interview may seem a little unprofessional at times.

He inserts a cigarette in an amber holder he's just taken out of his pocket and he lights it with a trembling hand. He returns the little book to the drawer he got it from and, to show that, in spite of everything, he hasn't lost the thread of my narrative, he again asks me what time it was when my mother gave me the fried eggs. I tell him that it would've been more or less half past four, and he twiddles the cigarette-holder between the thumb and forefinger of his right hand.

I suppose (he says) that by then your mother must've been feeling pretty tired. Particularly after spending the morning arguing.

Possibly (I accept), it's possible that she would've been tired by then, but Mother's a rather special case. She needs only a moment's rest to recover lost energy. She's a famous fighter, with unpredictable reactions, capable of surprising you with an unexpected sally. While I was eating, she was sunk in a state of deep dejection. She was seated in her armchair and, little by little, her expression was becoming more resigned. She seemed to be losing weight before my eyes and I even got the impression that, crushed by her afflictions, she could end up transformed into another of the cretonne's faded flowers. I'm referring, of course, to the cretonne which covered the armchair. It was a mistake, because when I approached to console her she nearly bit my finger. She straightened, as if activated by a spring, tightened her lips and gave me a look that made me retreat. At that moment it struck five and, hearing the chimes, she again asked at what time today I had my appointment with you. At two in the afternoon, I told her again. Then she said that two in the afternoon was not the most suitable time to make appointments, and that detail alone was enough to disqualify you. I asked her why and she replied that one ought to think twice about how much to trust an organization that showed so little respect for people's habits, making appointments with them at an hour traditionally set aside for the midday meal – lunch, that is – a tradition which helps to strengthen a dearly loved family break in the daily round.

Here's another proof of your lady mother's ingenuity

(cries Krugger, recovering his amused expression). Really, my friend, your mother's an exceptional person.

Yes, when it comes harping on something (I allow), my mother is exceptional. But I replied by telling her that this Bank, after all, was associated with a foreign Bank and it didn't have to bother about respecting some pretty absurd gastronomic habits.

Perfect, Krugger murmurs, more and more amused.

Then she got even more incensed (I go on) and, as a rejoinder, said that if this Bank was foreign, so much the worse, because working in a foreign enterprise meant guaranteed humiliation or, at least, countless misunderstandings. Then she made me take note that all the businesses with a majority of foreign capital which operated in this country were notorious for an exaggerated regard for money (that's what she thinks), that this goes much further than what can be considered morally admissible in a commercial establishment, that they should only be motivated by a reasonable level of profit. She even ventured to call them recalcitrant Calvinists. You must bear in mind that my mother has little sympathy for the foreigner.

Krugger is losing his smile little by little. He listens to me in silence, his head slightly on one side, as if at the same time as taking in my confidences he doesn't want to miss the persistent wheezing of his lungs.

You should have seen how she acted (I continue) when I said that nobody could be called guilty through the simple fact of having been born a few miles beyond our frontiers. She pointed her forefinger between my eyebrows, as if she were going to fire off a shot, and half-closed her eyelids in order to intensify her look. All right (she conceded, still pointing her finger at me), they're not to blame for being foreigners, but neither are we. So if they're foreigners, let them eat their own bread and not come bothering those who bear no blame for what they are. Then, a little calmer, she repeated that if I started to work in this Bank and didn't perform as they expected, they'd end up blaming the Inquisition.

Krugger smiles once more. He admits that his Bank has a majority of foreign capital (practically a hundred per cent), but that didn't mean that its ruling bodies (including, of course, its Board of Directors) did not feel and daily show a profound respect for this country's customs.

We feel (he adds) fully integrated into this society. Take me, for example. My name may not be very common here, but my mother was born barely five hundred yards from where we're sitting. Don't you think that makes me a very special sort of foreigner?

He defines himself as a type of hybrid, who rebels and even gets angry when someone criticizes his mother's country, and he alleges that a man who, from childhood, appreciates the merits of peppery salami, can never be called a foreigner.

I'm about to ask him how old he was when his mother died, so that I can draw my own conclusions, but he resumes his explanation before I can open my mouth. He mentions that his mother was a fervent xenophobe (like mine) in spite of being married to a foreigner, and that her main preoccupation was to ensure that her son (that is, himself) from his tenderest years identified with all of our country's values. He also explains to me that in order to achieve this objective she didn't hesitate in resorting to the most surprising methods and this was why (when Krugger was not yet five) he had to have for breakfast every morning a couple of fried eggs with peppery salami and half a glass of red wine.

He's told me all that with an indulgent smile and now he's silent, his chin sunk onto his chest, his gaze on the ashtray, as if there, changed into ash, were life's best memories. He's very little like the self-assured man who held out his hand to me when I entered this office. I can imagine him, against the grey background of the window (it's still raining slightly), in the park of some foggy central European city, rolling the hoop of his orphanhood without straying too far from an excessively strict governess. After a while he surfaces from his deep ruminations and sighs. He confesses that he'd give all the world's gold to have his mother back alive, although (as happens with me) he supposes there'd be some small co-existence problems. He looks at me enviously and shakes his head, as though regretting that things are as they are and not as they ought to be.

Who can ever forget his mother? (he exclaims, returning his gaze to the window). Mine, at least, is always present. There are even nights when, dreaming about her, I wake up startled and then feel she's right beside me, scolding me for something I've done or not done during the day.

He's silent again, lulled by his sibilant breathing, and for the first time I wonder about the hidden reason for his fits of nostalgia. I'm in quite a delicate position. After all, I came into this office looking for employment and I can't run the risk of adopting a wrong attitude. What's the best thing for me to do in these circumstances? Become sad as well? Share his melancholy mood? Look out of the window and weep for the joys of days gone by? Or, on the contrary, should I try to rouse his spirits, telling him that, in spite of everything, life is something that deserves to be lived happily?

I imagine (he says at last, reacting feebly) that you won't now think I'm one of those recalcitrant Calvinists your mother so hates.

Of course not (I hasten to reply), I've nothing against foreigners. When my mother brought up the Inquisition theme, I told her it was time this country began to recognize its own faults and to be less arrogant, because some good things had been done beyond our borders, too. What? she asked me. The French Revolution, for example (I replied). It was the first thing that occurred to me, but my mother, a monarchist to the marrow, called me Robespierre. That's right (I exclaimed) I'm the Robespierre who's spent thirty years watching his mother knit. Then, getting back to our argument's departure point, I told her that quite apart from what I was or might be, foreigners didn't have to bother about our gastronomic inclinations which, anyway, seemed pretty silly to me also. It may be (I granted) that in this country we've been big in metaphysics and similar abstractions, but it's definitely others who discovered the art of making money. So it seems to me absolutely right for those important financiers to laugh at our anachronistic meals, with their three courses, coffee, brandy and cigar.

What did she say to that? (Krugger asks).

She didn't know how to respond (I reply) and went on bringing up fresh arguments. I observed that the fact that you'd given me an appointment at two o'clock could be viewed positively, if it was seen as attempt to eradicate from this country deplorable habits such as those enormous spreads that dull the senses, and those outdated siestas from which one awakes hating one's neighbour even more.

3

You, I repeat (interrupts Krugger, pointing his finger at me), talk like a book. You said earlier that your mother took you out of school and, from then on, personally took charge of your education. Was it she who taught you to talk in this fashion?

I tell him it was, that since I was ten she'd been my only teacher, but he doesn't seem convinced. He almost certainly suspects I'm a man of wide and well chosen reading, but he doesn't immediately insist on further explanation. He raises his eyebrows and pushes out his lower lip, while his right hand creeps towards the packet of cigarettes he has on the table.

Anyway, (he adds), your ideas about the siesta I find highly debatable. I personally think it's an admirable custom, although, unfortunately, I'm unable to observe it.

He looks out of the window again, as if he felt attracted by the rain, and he asks me to continue.

My sticking up for foreigners (I go on) put my mother out of countenance and she shut herself up in her room. We thus established a kind of truce. It would have then been about six or half past, and I took advantage of her absence to try to finish the crossword I'd begun earlier. Ten minutes later, however, she came back into the dining-room, drying her eyes with a handkerchief, as if to tell me she'd spent all that time crying. She sat down again in her armchair and looked at me fixedly, perhaps hoping I'd say something from which she could extract some comfort. I was on the point of going off to the other end of the house to show her I had nothing new to say and that I considered the discussion closed, but once again I decided it was better to keep her company, if only to demonstrate that I wasn't frightened of her and that I was quite prepared to meet all her attacks with reasoned argument. So that's what I did and for a good while, as night was falling, we sat without exchanging a single word. We ended up in the dark, with no light other than the greenish glare that filtered in from the balcony. I'm referring to the glare from the neon light, advertising the delicatessen we have on the other side of the street. When I turned on the light, I discovered her sunk in her chair, with an air of never having said boo to a goose. She immediately began to snivel, but seeing that I took no notice, she let her handkerchief fall to the floor, to give me the opportunity, when picking it up, of saying something at the same time. Do you see? Like an offended *fiancée*. The way *fiancées* used to be.

Did you pick it up? Krugger inquires.

I didn't lift a finger (I reply). I sat there with one leg crossed over the other. She then redoubled her tears, but stopped immediately when the telephone began to ring. I started to get up, but sank back with a gesture, remembering that it was still her house and that she, therefore, should be the one to answer. We've got the phone at the end of the passage, in the hall. Well, she went off to answer, leaving the dining-room, and a moment later I heard her cry out in the passage. I was startled, went to see what was happening and found her on the floor, trying to get up. She'd slipped. It wasn't a

serious fall, but she acted up. Whining a bit, she told me
she'd broken her arm, but I immediately saw she was
putting on another of her productions. I picked her up
and carried her to her bed. She went on complaining for
quite a while, repeating amid moans that she felt near
her end. I asked her if she wanted me to call the doctor
and she said no, that all she wanted was to die, because
all that she'd had to do in this world had already been
done.

Krugger is listening to me now with a glassy, abstract
expression, as if my mother's slip had awakened painful
memories. I go on to tell him that, after laying her on
the bed, I threw a blanket over her and sat down by the
headboard.

After a little while (I recall) she stopped moaning
and lay there quietly, gazing at the ceiling, her mouth
half-open, as if fancying herself dead, but occasionally
checking out of the corner of her eye to see if I was still
there. I'd better call the doctor, I said. I started to get
up, but she caught me by the arm, forgetting her dying
act. She sat up, resting her elbows on the pillow and
confessed that what hurt most was not her arm but the
displeasure I was giving her, and that the only doctor
who could cure that was myself. She also said she wasn't
denying me the right to go out occasionally for a stroll
round the neighbourhood, but what made her cross
was my stubbornness about starting work, exposing
myself to nine or ten hours a day among people we
didn't know. She added that God helped those who
faced danger through necessity, but not those who did
so capriciously. How can you possibly not understand?
she cried out, sitting straight up now and clasping my
hands.

A dramatic situation, Krugger murmurs.

It certainly was (I agree), and the truth is that I didn't immediately know how to get out of it. I said I'd better get back to the dining-room to finish the crossword I'd left half-undone, and she collapsed again. That's all I need (she moaned), here I am dying and you're thinking about crosswords. But seeing that I wasn't saying sorry, she again asked: How can you possibly not understand? Then I said yes, I understood her and that perhaps God didn't help those who capriciously courted danger, but that neither could a man spend his life lifting up every stone he found on the way, to check whether a scorpion was hiding beneath it. I made this observation in the tone of one talking to a child and went on sitting by the top of the bed. So you can see: nobody could accuse me of lack of patience.

Certainly not (Krugger agrees), you're definitely a patient son. But don't boast: sons can never congratulate themselves on being patient with their mothers. When you come down to it, a man's worth is related to the respect he shows those who brought him into this world.

The fact is (I continue, without embroiling myself in an argument, but standing by my ideas) that I'm not resigned to my mother's continuing to use me as a doormat. Nor am I resigned to her egoism. So, while she lay in bed complaining, I came out with a long speech about one's fellow men. I appealed to her sense of solidarity and said that in these present times nobody can afford the luxury of living in an ivory tower. I reminded her that while we had a full larder there were people begging in the street, bombs exploding, businesses crashing and the number of unemployed constantly increasing. I noted that disorder was becoming more and more general and that every day, because of the prevailing doubt, more and more men weren't even sure what sex they belonged to. I said all this respectfully but do you know what she did?

No, Krugger whispers.

She covered her head with the blanket (I tell him), she didn't want to listen to me any more, and I found that extremely rude. I removed the blanket and, without changing tone, went on talking about the people who needed our help in one way or another. I said that we couldn't live shut up in our little world, looking at ourselves in a house-trained mirror which only reflects the image we want to see.

Krugger crosses his arms and concentrates his gaze on the small glass cube which he uses as a paperweight. He slowly turns over the ideas in his mind, as if they were cooking over a low flame and finally allows (with the resigned air of one who has to admit that summer is over at last) that I'm not wrong to think that no man should live isolated from the world, indifferent and alien to it, just enjoying his own happiness and without wanting to think about his fellow men.

Looking at things from this angle (he adds), I recognize that you would be of more use to your neighbour working in this Bank than staying all day shut up inside the four walls of your house. When you come down to it, banks generate wealth for everybody. However, we can't afford to run the risk of excessive sentimentality or unhealthy philanthropy.

What do you mean by unhealthy philanthropy? I ask him.

You know perfectly well (he replies). You know very well that even the best sentiments, if elevated beyond reasonable limits, can lead to regrettable errors. Concern for one's neighbours has my approval, but not to the point of wearing their shoes.

Let's clarify things (I suggest, trying to recover lost ground), don't you agree that now is the time to open our hearts to those who haven't the luck to be loved? Do we have to go on being encapsulated within our own impoverished spirits? What could my mother and I achieve, living as we have? A few more years of calm, humdrum happiness? All right, I agree. But what would happen afterwards, when the mist which now surrounds us dispels? What world shall we find ourselves in? What kind of desolate universe? And another thing: let's imagine that everything works out well and that the world ends up righting itself without our help. Tell me: what right would we then have to enjoy the renewed beauty of gardens? What right would we have to inhale the perfume of resurrected flowers?

Krugger's eyes now look grey. He reflects on what he's just heard and then says, slowly, that he can no longer allow me to go on deceiving him and he accuses me of being an educated man. And much more educated than could be considered suitable in a night watchman. If it wasn't so (he suggests, stroking the paperweight), how could you talk about the renewed beauty of gardens or the perfume of resurrected roses?

It looks as if he is slowly beginning to take my mother's side. He's concentrating on my mouth and I'm feeling uncomfortable, as if he'd just uncovered a grave, secret sin. I've no alternative but to admit that I like reading. In fact (I confess, with my eyes on the floor) that's all I've done in my life: read.

Do you think (I ask him) I could have put up with so many years of loneliness in any other way?

Krugger shakes his head sadly. He stops playing with the glass paperweight and joins the fingertips of his hands together. He makes no attempt to hide his annoyance. He pauses, then sighs deeply. He admits that he's found some estimable qualities in me, but the fact of my being an educated man (he tells me quite frankly) may reduce my application's chance of success.

Don't run away thinking the men of this Bank aren't aware of the advantages of culture (he tries to justify himself), but culture (and I'm not happy about having to admit this) can sometime be counter-productive. Shakespeare's poems, to give an example, could be politically suspect on the lips of a simple nightwatchman.

Who was this Shakespeare? I ask him, defensively.

He starts shaking his head again and says that he's sure that I know very well who Shakespeare was. He's even certain that I've read *The Divine Comedy*, which is the best of his tragedies. Here's another of his clumsy tricks, I tell myself. But I'm not so naïve as to correct him. I cross my arms (it's the first time I've allowed myself this position since entering his office) and try to take things philosophically. Krugger, meanwhile, goes on justifying himself. He says that the ideas about culture which a banking establishment can allow itself revolve around certain considerations of a practical nature and he asks me what guarantee a guard could give his Bank, or any other bank, that, at the very moment of pressing the trigger of his pistol against an attacker, he wouldn't suddenly remember a sonnet, and freeze?

Moreover (he goes on to tell me), there's something else which worries me: someone who lies once can lie again. You said earlier that you didn't like music, but I now find that hard to believe. You like music, in the same way that you like reading. They're two tastes that usually go together. It may even be that everything you've said about your lady mother has been a lie. Perhaps the portrait of her you've painted is only a montage, so that we overvalue your eagerness to become independent and consider your application with special sympathy. Tell me, my friend, is your mother only an invention?

Do you think (I protest) mothers can be invented?

He acknowledges my words with a wan smile and, without transition, again falls into a fit of melancholy. He stretches his hand towards the glass paperweight, but quickly changes his mind and lights up a fresh cigarette. It seems as if every now and then he sees himself obliged to open the window of memory on to an ancient landscape populated by sorrows. He's silently reclining in his chair, his gaze lost in space, but even so, I can't allow myself the luxury of dropping my guard. I'm also inclined to be distrustful; it's possible that silence is now being prolonged only to see if I'm capable of taking the initiative.

What, exactly, is the required level of initiative for a bank's nightwatchman? It would cost me little to reopen the conversation on some pretext or other (mentioning the rain, for example, or the paintings that decorate the walls of the office), but what if he considers that such worldly expedients are not suitable in a good guard? And what if he brands me as being frivolous or disrespectful? So I keep my mouth shut and, at last, Krugger envelops me in a gaze which plainly shows how much effort's required to come back to the present.

You and I (he whispers) know very well that it wasn't Shakespeare who wrote *The Divine Comedy*.

He gives a sudden start, sits up straight and, with his elbows on the table, confesses that he, too, likes reading and that not a weekend goes by without his reading at least a couple of books. His eyes brighten and he tries to gauge what effect his revelation has on me, but I'm not running the risk of showing surprise. I accept his confession as a logical fact and I'm interested in the type of reading he prefers. Above all, poetry, he whispers. He casts a fearful look around the room to check that nobody else has heard him, and we sit there silently, looking each other in the eye, like two early Christians who, among a throng of infidels, suddenly recognize one another for what they are.

Then he requests discretion. He says that, after all, he belongs to the staff of the Bank and that for obvious reasons he can't do without his employment. He's obliged to abide in secrecy; in a certain way, he belongs to secret poetry. They could accuse me of being a fifth-columnist, he murmurs, smiling sadly.

I'm not completely convinced of his sincerity and I continue to keep up my guard. The rain has lessened and the sun, behind a light cloak of clouds, is spreading a saffron-coloured splendour over the firmament. Krugger understands my reserve and justifies his confidences. He tells me that he now sees me, not as a possible Bank employee, but as a like-minded person with whom he can share his sorrows and longings and even his most secret interests.

What's certain (he continues) is that your talking so much about your mother, makes me think about mine. In a certain way, all mothers are alike. They belong to the same clan.

Do you think (I ask him) yours wouldn't have let you work either?

Maybe not (he whispers). Maybe she wouldn't have allowed me to. Or perhaps yes, who knows. Many years have gone by since I saw her for the last time.

He confesses that his mother died in an accident. One of those silly accidents with fatal consequences that can, overnight, change the course of our lives. Krugger recalls that his family lived in a two-storeyed house at that time. One morning, coming out of her room, his mother stepped on some chick-peas, slipped and fell downstairs.

I was playing marbles in the drawing-room (he goes on recalling, while gazing at the ashtray). I heard her screams, ran to her side and found her with her eyes blank and her head split open.

I don't utter a word. Any misjudged expression of condolence could be counter-productive. I restrict myself to moving my head and Krugger adds that the accident wasn't entirely clear and that, at the request of one of his uncles (his mother's brother), the police intervened. He says that his mother (like all illustrious ladies of her time) was fairly harsh with the servants, and that it was thought the accident (apparently fortuitous) could have been brought about by a resentful servant.

Suspicion fell on the cook (he recalls), whom a maid had surprised that same morning at a very early hour, scattering chick-peas on the stairway. But it wasn't possible to prove anything and the case was closed.

He wipes his hand across his brow and sighs. I imagine him sitting beside his mother's lifeless body, bewildered by the servants' concert of cries. I also think about the suspected cook (perhaps she wasn't scattering the fateful chick-peas, but picking them up) and I have a vague premonition which fades away before it can materialize into a concrete idea. It's like one of those films which roll too rapidly and in which the most revealing image (capable on its own of uncovering the whole mystery) has passed before we've had time to understand it at a conscious level.

He's continuing to lean against the back of his chair, with an absent look and the index finger of his right hand pressed between his eyebrows, but I go on thinking it would be a mistake to give him my sympathy forty or fifty years after the event, and to break the silence (which was beginning to be oppressive), I clear my throat and start to generalize about the wide variety of ways in

which it pleases fate to strike at a man. I tell him also
that the devil is often disguised as a lamb and that the
smallest things (a couple of chick-peas, for example) can
be the cause of the greatest tragedies.

He makes no comment. He sprawls even more in his
seat and lights another cigarette. I'm sure that, if she
were still alive, his mother wouldn't allow him to smoke
so much. He keeps the holder tightly clamped between
his teeth and the smoke, escaping from the corners of
his mouth, forces him to narrow his eyes. I'm not put off
and I mention some accidents whose victims didn't even
have the luck to die quickly.

At least your mother died without suffering (I say).

His silence continues but the wheezing of his lungs
rises an octave. He seems to have forgotten that he has
in front of him a man who, after all, came into this office
with the sole purpose of being given a job. It's true I,
too, could keep my mouth shut now, but I can't rule out
the possibility that, by revealing his troubles and appearing so downcast, he's not trying to check how sincere I
was a moment ago when I talked about the need to share
our neighbour's unhappiness.

It doesn't seem wise, therefore, to adopt a distant
approach, but nor do I want to embark on a series of
condolences which may seem to him purely perfunctory.
It looks as if the most suitable course is to go on digres-
sing about the benefits of resignation. I tell him that when
one door shuts another opens, that pain is the best path
to inner perfection and that I'm sure his mother continues to watch over him from the other world. I finally
get him to give me a grateful look. He takes the holder
from his mouth, coughs slightly and his chest crackles
like a roast chestnut. He's about to say something but
at this precise moment the telephone rings. His hand

flies to the receiver and he gets involved in a long conversation. He's employing a language I don't recognize, and the office is filled with strange and exotic inflexions. Krugger, after some hesitant openings, is expressing himself more and more forthrightly. His look is becoming progressively brighter, as if fed by some inner battery that, little by little, is recharging itself. He nods his head energetically, contracts his jaw and spasmodically opens and shuts his right hand on top of the desk. He ends up cutting his words as if with a knife and triumphantly hurling them down the phone. His transformation fills me with anxiety and suspicion. He's become a different man, barely recalling the grieving gentleman who, only a moment ago, was crushed by the memory of a mother who's been dead for half a century.

Which of the two Kruggers is the real one? I ask myself.

I'm now seeing him at the centre of a world of steely efficiency, in which there's no room for obsessive mothers or, as he himself said earlier, unhealthy philanthropy. This man has never read a poem, I suspect, as he lets loose a loud laugh at the person he's talking to. Suddenly and unavoidably, I feel like an intruder who has blundered without warning into a temple dedicated to strange cults. What if my mother were right? I ask myself. What if, today, I've imprudently crossed the first dangerous threshold of my life?

He hangs up the phone at last and is quiet for a moment, perhaps savouring his success. Finally he tells me that he's just been speaking to the Chairman of the Management Committee. The Chairman's congratulated him on information he supplied some days back. Sometimes (he explains to me, as if justifying himself) an unexpected voice reaches us, restoring our confidence and encouraging us to go on living.

He clicks his tongue, reflects and adds that, yes, life

is something that is worth living. Partly referring to his previous nostalgia, he confesses that his superiors' esteem is the best compensation a man like him can have, a man who's devoted body and soul to his workplace, but who, at the personal level, lacks loved ones with whom he can share daily griefs and joys. He lights another cigarette (although the previous one is still burning in the ashtray) and, smiling indulgently, defines himself as the perfect bachelor who doesn't even have any brothers and sisters, or nieces and nephews.

Well (he sighs, consulting his wristwatch), carry on talking. Take up your story from the moment when you spoke to your mother about the resurrection of roses. Do you really believe dead roses can be revived?

My mother (I continue) finally went to sleep and I took advantage of the occasion to slip outside for a stroll round the neighbourhood. It would've been about eight, and for the next half hour I sat on a bench in the small park some two hundred yards from our house, which was opened something like a couple of months ago. I tried, in the moonlight, to put my mind in order and, more or less an hour later, I went back home, prepared – if I found my mother awake – to put up with her grumbles about my going out without having first let her know.

4

The telephone rings again. This time his interlocutor doesn't even give him time to reply and from the very beginning Krugger starts to nod rapidly. He lets out several 'yes, sirs', 'of course, sirs', 'naturally, sirs' and, when the other end cuts short the monotonous whispering, he hangs up the receiver with a deeply moved expression. This time it's the Director General who has phoned. It's as though the chief executives of the Bank had all agreed to remind him that, in spite of all, he's an important man. He tells me that the Director General has just shown yet again that he has complete confidence in his professional competence.

That excellent gentleman (he says) isn't too satisfied with his present secretary and he's asked me to find him another one by next week. The ideal woman (he adds, winking at me). You must know what I mean.

It's evident he's regained all his self-confidence and that, his period of depression overcome, he's again feeling permeated by the importance of his post. He opens the top drawer of his desk, takes the photos of four girls from a folder and arranges them on top of the table so that all four can be seen at a glance. Then he changes the order, puts his head on one side to see them from another angle and finally raises his eyebrows. Which would you choose? he asks, showing me them.

I don't know how to reply. I point to a short-haired blonde and he tells me we agree, that the girl has the most exciting face, but that her measurements (which he has noted down on the back of the photo) aren't ideal. At least, they aren't what the Director likes. In the end, he settles for a dark-haired girl with a defiant attitude. Besides having suitable measurements, she's a passable typist (that point is also covered on the back of the photo), with the least spelling mistakes.

I don't want to lose the chance of being amusing and I say that his Director General must be one of those old lechers with a liking for pinching secretaries' bottoms. My observation surprises him, but he makes no comment. He returns the rejected photos to the folder and puts the selected one in an envelope. He presses a button he has on the side of the desk and finally comments that what I've said seems out of place to him and that I shouldn't have spoken so recklessly about a person whom, quite clearly, I did not know.

I don't exactly know why you think our Director General is an old lecher (he says), but in any case it should be obvious to you that, beneath the most frivolous attitude, the greatest complexity can be hidden – and a man with the highest sense of responsibility.

I feel humiliated. I'm on the point of asking why he winked at me and what he meant me to understand when he did so. But I prefer to hold my tongue. It's not in my interest to provoke gratuitous confrontation and I decide that the best course in the circumstances is to apologize or, at least, to give him some explanation. With a humble smile, I suggest that to call a man an old lecher mustn't always be interpreted pejoratively, because, after all, it implies a certain youthful vitality and drive, virtues that shouldn't be limited to the world of sex exclusively, but extended also to that of work and to any other essential activity.

He purses his lips, as if my words have only half-convinced him. A messenger comes into the office, collects the envelope and goes back towards the door with the respectful, springy step of those who leave a shrine conscious that the altar is behind their back. I go on to tell Krugger that I know very well that nobody can make fun of a mature man just because he likes women, since their charms (women's charms, obviously) are so many and so varied that they justify whatever weakness.

Do you really believe all you say? he interrupts, looking straight at me.

I feel disconcerted and don't know how to reply. I blush and avoid his eyes. I wasn't expecting an attack from that direction. At last I manage to say that, of course, round about that age men lose their heads over a pair of pretty legs. This means I'm only half-replying to his question and he's not convinced. In fact, it wouldn't have convinced anybody. He shakes his head from side to side and considers that a man like me shouldn't speak in that way and shouldn't resort to such subjects.

After all (he adds in justification), you've never had a woman in your arms.

What's happening doesn't seem fair to me. I came into this office seeking employment and intending to answer all the questions put to me honestly, not to undergo a session of psychoanalysis. There are certain situations a man can't accept with folded arms; so I decide to stake all on a single card. I look him in the eye and admit that he is right, that I've never had a woman in my arms, but that is precisely why he and I are condemned to understand each other.

Because you, Sir (I say, raising my head a little higher) don't know what a woman is either.

I don't at this moment care if he flies in a rage and says the interview's over. It doesn't matter if he sends me packing. I want to make it quite clear that I'm a man who knows the correct response. So now it's I who do the straight looking, until I see him lower his gaze. He clears his throat, stretches his right hand out to stroke the telephone (it's an instinctive gesture that reflects his inner turmoil) and says nothing. It's clear I've scored a bull's-eye. He coughs again and finally recovers the power of speech. He says he prefers us to shelve the subject of women because we are getting into private territory and personal intimacies that have nothing to do with the purpose of the interview.

In any case (he determines), what is of interest is your private life, not mine. It's you who've come to this office with the aim of being given a job.

In a conciliatory tone he adds that, quite apart from our private lives, it doesn't seem right to slight the Bank's Director General, because he looks upon himself as a loyal employee and he can't forget the enormous amount – ignoring his innocent flirtations – that man has done for the Institution.

Nevertheless, I'm not going to allow him to recover so easily.

Do you believe (I ask) that a Bank official who spends his weekends reading poems can call himself a loyal employee?

I'm sure he regrets having confided in me. He looks round the room and wrinkles his brow. There's too much smoke in here, he whispers. He gets up and opens the window wide. A gust of wind, which turns the leaves of a calendar he has on top of the desk, swirls into the room. It's raining hard again and I can see a procession of low clouds slowly advancing from the North. Standing in front of the window, Krugger exposes his lungs to the humid air, as if he had the overriding need to feel alive again, after what I'd said to him. He breathes in deeply, rhythmically flexing his shoulders and throwing his head back with each intake of air. After a while, he closes the window and when he returns to his seat behind the desk I no longer see any traces of ill-feeling in his expression.

It may even be that my application now has more chance of success because he knows I've discovered his double Achilles heel: a loneliness, which nobody can really be blamed for, and, more pertinently, his liking for poetry which, if discovered, could mean the end of his Bank career.

I think it'll be best if we get on with our business (he murmurs). Your lady mother slipped in the passage and you carried her to her bedroom, laid her on the bed and threw a blanket over her. She ended up going to sleep and then you went out for a stroll round the neighbour-hood. That's what you told me. What happened next? Did you get the ticking-off you feared for having gone out without permission?

On the contrary (I say), I found her up, but she wel-comed me with a kiss on the forehead. She said we were going to celebrate. Just the two of us. She'd get everything ready. All I had to do was to put on the clothes she'd laid out on the bed. She also asked me to comb my hair in the way men had it fifty years ago. Once I'd done all that, I had to wait in my room till she told me to come out. I didn't raise any objections: my mother's a capri-cious woman who's always had her own way, but, last night, I decided it was the last time I was putting up with her nonsense. I went to my room and found a dark blue suit, a white shirt and a pearl grey tie. They had all belonged to my father. The suit was too tight and I could hardly button the shirt collar. When I was ready, I sat

down on the bed and heard her hurried footsteps around
the house for quite a while. I was beginning to repent of
having lent myself to this charade. Finally she summoned
me. I went to the dining-room and found her in her chair,
wearing her black silk dress, the one for formal occasions, and half a dozen imitation necklaces.

Krugger's face lights up. He crosses his arms and looks
at the ceiling, as if he could picture my mother's appearance better in that posture.

The first thing I thought (I continue) was that she'd
put on too much make-up. I had the feeling of having
stumbled upon an apparition emerged from some old
fashion-magazine. I was dumbfounded, I didn't know
what to say, partly nauseated by the smell of camphor
from so many old clothes. Maybe she was expecting some
compliment, but seeing that I wasn't saying anything,
she stretched out her hand to me so that I could kiss it.
From the depth of her chair she looked at me with a rapt
expression and said that, what with wearing that suit
and, especially, with my hair in that fashion, I was my
father's living portrait. I still didn't know what to say. I
limited myself to kissing her hand, but I believe that then,
to show her somehow how much I was impressed by
her appearance, I gave her a military salute, the way soldiers salute old regimental colours carried in procession.

Where did you do your military service? (Krugger suddenly enquires). In the infantry? In the navy?

I find it a stupid question at this stage. I remind him
I'm a widow's son and, therefore, free from military service. He frowns and notes that this circumstance is going
to make the success of my application more difficult,
because it suggests that I've never used a firearm.

What's that got to do with my job in this Bank? I
exclaim.

This Bank (he replies) prefers to recruit its guards from candidates who have experience in the handling of firearms.

And amplifying his answer, he tells me that for most people military service affords the only opportunity they ever have of squeezing a trigger.

Personally (he adds) this criterion seems to me a reasonable one, because firing a gun or pistol for the first time is always a traumatizing experience.

I don't understand what he means exactly, and he explains further. In his opinion (and in the opinion of the Bank for which he works), firearms offer us the magic of being able to kill at a distance, without physical contact with our victims.

That magic (he observes) has not always been assimilated properly by those shooting for the first time.

He notices my puzzlement and, so that I can better understand, he gets lost in confusing marginal reflections about the arsenal at man's disposal throughout the ages. He emphasizes man's innate ability to handle a cudgel (one is dealing with a basic skill inherent in all mortals and transmitted in the genes from father to son throughout countless generations) and he underlines the circumstances in which swords (which, like clubs, are held by one end) can also be thought of as pointed sticks.

You must understand (he says with a smile) that, if our Bank's guards were armed with swords, the fact that you've not done military service wouldn't matter to us at all. Pistols, however, are what they use. A work tool which, however much you argue about it, consists of a number of very sophisticated parts. You have, for example, the shell's mercury fulminate, or even the simple powder which revolutionized the art of war. The handling of pistols, therefore, demands not only a certain familiarity and a minimum level of skill, but also an adequate technical knowledge which people doing their military service usually acquire.

It's hard for me to believe that he's said all this seriously and I look him straight in the eye, ready to guffaw the moment he makes it clear he's joking and testing my good faith. But his face is an inexpressive mask.

Well it's a pity (I say at last, hoping he'll pick up my irony) that this Bank's guards can't make do with clubs.

You know very well that's not possible (he argues), because assailants carry pistols. They even use shorn-off shotguns. Don't you think it's logical that guards, defending this Bank, should employ means proportionate to those utilized by the aggressor?

I agree with a quick nod and Krugger's face brightens slightly. He adds that there's another reason which justifies and even calls for the use of firearms, and it's related to the Bank's prestige: in these times of the apotheosis of information techniques, of sophisticated networks of telecommunications and of electronic money, it would be quite absurd to see any bank's guards armed with clubs.

As you can imagine (he says, smiling), it's also a matter of corporate image.

I'm still looking him in the eye, marvelling at his reasons. Three explanations occur to me right away:

First – That he's magnifying my inexperience with firearms, so that he can later justify the failure of my application.

Second – That, in spite of his serious delivery, he's pulling my leg.

Third – That he's mad or, at the very least, he's suffering from one of those fits of madness that sometimes surface from the depths of our consciousness.

I try to take things philosophically and say that I can

always learn how to shoot a pistol and to forget what I've read in books these last few years.

That's not so easy as you think, he replies, shaking his head several times.

His air of condescension is now insulting. He's lost his early warmth. He's sitting upright in the chair, with his forearms on the desk top and the tips of his fingers touching, while, at his back, rain goes on pelting against the window-panes. He's looking at me full in the face, but I get the impression that his blue eyes are going straight through me, claimed by other more important business somewhere further off.

I want to believe that his attitude is purely a mask to hide the uneasiness he feels sitting opposite a man who has uncovered some of his secrets. As he doesn't say anything, I interpret his silence as an unspoken invitation to proceed with my narrative.

Well (I continue), as I say, my mother in her chair received me with the air of a queen. She'd set the table as if it were Christmas, with a linen tablecloth, a silver candlestick with red candles and chinaware, with a motif of roses, which I hadn't seen before. She asked me to bring the gramophone and records from the storeroom and to put them on top of the cupboard, with the loudspeaker facing a corner. You'll probably remember those old loudspeakers which looked like flowers. When I had everything ready, she gave me permission to sit at the head of the table. It was the first time I sat in the place that had belonged to my father and which, until yesterday, I'd always seen empty. She left me on my own and five minutes later came back from the kitchen with a tray in each hand. While I was out, the poor thing had cooked a superlative supper. She made another journey to the fridge and returned with a couple of bottles of champagne. Smiling, I asked if her arm was still hurting and, returning my smile, she said that, right then, she didn't want to have arms, she wanted only heart and nostalgia. She pulled the balcony curtains, lit the candles, put on the gramophone, and a small, insubstantial voice pierced the air, quickly getting caught up in impassioned arabesques.

Krugger interrupts: A tango?

My mother's favourite tango, I reply.

I find tangos fascinating, he whispers, stroking the knot of his tie with his index finger.

His expression softens, he withdraws his hands from the table and sits with his arms crossed, smiling slightly. He tells me that he remembers those old, bygone gramophones very well, that his mother had one also and that, indeed, it had a loudspeaker like the corolla of a flower.

While the record was playing (I go on) my mother uncorked a bottle of champagne, filled our glasses to the brim and we began our supper without speaking.

Krugger now asks me what my mother had done for supper, but I've reached the point where none of his questions surprise me. I tell him she served turbot in lemon sauce, with white rice, one of my favourite dishes, and I see him smile wanly.

If you don't mind my being frank (he says in a slightly bantering tone), that sounds like too sophisticated a supper: I can't imagine one of our nightwatchmen sitting down to a plate of turbot in lemon sauce.

He adds that there's something else he doesn't quite understand: he can't see how my mother had time to prepare such a complicated dish in the brief hour I was out of the house. I reply telling him that the turbot had been bought five days earlier, that I remember going with my mother to the market that morning, and that since then it had been in the freezer.

What's more (I emphasize), preparing turbot in lemon sauce isn't complicated. All you have to do is boil the fish and, also, boil a bit of rice.

Krugger denies this, vehemently shaking his head. He resorts to his mother's old recipe book and opens at page T.

What about peeling the tomatoes? (he asks me, without looking up from the tiny handwriting). And cutting them open, removing the pulp and cutting them into small slices? What about washing, draining and dicing the parsley? And what about making the lemon sauce, with its sugar, paprika, yoghurt and mayonnaise base?

Like so many bachelors, he must be a demanding gourmet, fond of doing his own cooking. I know there are solid men who aren't ashamed of talking about divine hams and unforgettable cheeses. He goes on shaking his head, puts the book back in the drawer and sarcastically suggests that my mother's turbot was really a sardine. I find his remark in bad taste, even bordering on rudeness, but I don't want to start an argument, because it may be he's trying to find a way of provoking me.

So I restrict myself to repeating that my mother's an excellent cook and that she had plenty of time to get supper ready while I was out. Krugger looks at the drawer again and I'm momentarily afraid he's going to read me all his mother's recipes to prove she was a better cook than mine. In the end, he just shrugs his shoulders and asks me to continue. He's interested to know what I spoke to my mother about during supper.

In effect (I tell him), she was the only one who spoke. She talked about thousands of things: her interests when she was single, her childhood friends, how elegant my father looked in the same suit I was wearing (which was barely letting me breathe), double-decker trams, cock-fights...As you see, she was referring to things that had nothing to do with each other, with me not opening my mouth and with her not showing the slightest interest in learning what my opinion might be. We finished the first bottle of champagne (she drank more than half), uncorked the second and, from then on, she spoke exclusively about my father. She remembered his manliness, his way of smiling, his fiery glance and, above all, the deep love that united them during their five years of marriage.

Did you know your father? asks Krugger.

He died before I was four, (I answer), but my mother often used to talk to me about him. But last night she was really exaggerating. She was depicting him as though he'd been a kind of god. While I was doing justice to the turbot (or whatever it was, which, when you come down to it, isn't all that important), she was piling on the compliments. Then, lifting her champagne glass, she drank his health and told me once again that I was my father's living portrait and that it was as if he went on living in me.

Krugger smiles. He also thinks that, in a way, parents are made immortal by their children. He recalls that his, like mine, were married for five years. Then he leans back in his chair and is silent. There is no serenity in his expression, however. Some inner tension turns down the corners of his mouth and, every now and then, the whistling of his lungs becomes more urgent, like a train's whistle as it approaches an unmanned level-crossing.

Do you believe (he suddenly asks me) that mothers always end up forgiving their children?

It's another of his stupid questions. I reply that mine has nothing to forgive, that it's I who have quite a lot to forgive her.

Doesn't it seem to you (he goes on to ask me, ignoring my previous reply) that mothers always love their children and that they never tire of being mothers?

Let's assume it's as you say, I reply, without committing myself.

My reply doesn't satisfy him and he goes on looking straight at me, waiting for me to say something else. I don't do so and my silence ends up annoying him. He says, getting increasingly excited, that mothers catch hold of knives by their blades rather than have their children hurt themselves and that, even if their children are snakes, they let them crawl all over them. To emphasize his words, he raises his right hand and talks about the pelican, the symbol of maternal love, which sprinkles its dead chicks with its own blood in an attempt to bring them back to life.

It doesn't even matter to them (he pronounces) if their children are murderers.

I can't help smiling. I say that it's not so bad as all that, that my mother's no pelican and I'm no murderer, and that, in my opinion, things are getting out of hand. Krugger shakes his head and smiles in a mysterious, distant manner, jutting out his lower lip. He emphasizes that he wasn't specifically thinking of my case and that he was speaking generally, but that my mother, from what I'd said, could be called a symbol of maternal love, taken to its ultimate extremes.

Well I still haven't told you everything (I continue, picking up the thread). The most pathetic part came later, after supper. You can probably imagine it: we were sitting in our respective chairs and she was continuing to come out with a string of reminiscences with the half-defeated and half-resigned air of one who expects nothing good out of life. She ended up shedding a few tears, which made her eye make-up run. Then, nostalgia took over and she asked me to put a pasodoble on the gramophone to raise her spirits. It was a mistake on her part, because, listening to that pasodoble (sung by an invert who, it appears, was in fashion thirty years ago), I realized that what she was proposing was to keep me in a decaying world, without any chance of resurrection. A world that was completely dead. You wonder why I understood she was proposing that completely dead world? For a very simple reason: because the old homosexual on the record was singing with his voice in his throat, and with the hissing and emphasis usual in that kind of artist, but at the same time with a certain blatancy and, occasionally, brazenness which I found gratuitous, accentuating every strong vowel and quite shamelessly round the o's, as if he wanted to show the men of his epoch (who almost certainly mocked him mercilessly and had him run a gauntlet of stones in the street) that, if it came to it, he could be as masculine as they. It was like listening to a feeble mazurka. Do you follow me?

Perfectly (Krugger affirms). I'd go as far as to say that those unfortunate pansies had no choice but to sing in that way if they wanted to survive. They were like exotic flowers that bravely displayed their petals amid an uncompromising *machista* society. In a certain sense, if you'll forgive me the contradiction, they virilely exaggerated their homosexual nature.

Well (I continue), that record came to an end and back we went to an interminable series of tangos. It was genuine torture which I patiently bore, saying to myself over and over again that it was the last whim I was allowing her. I was so fed up with accordions that I asked if she had any other records by the brazen pansy, but at that precise moment her favourite tango began to play. Do you know what she did then?

How could I? Krugger whispers.

Her mouth like a rosebud, she asked me to invite her to dance. All right (I said), let's dance, but don't complain if I tread on your feet. She said it didn't matter, that all she wanted was to dance with me. It was quite ludicrous. I felt like the romantic lead in one of those silent movies where the actors always end up throwing custard pies at each other. At every turn my mother (in spite of her arthritis) bent from the waist, languidly throwing herself backwards. I soon got tired and, using a stumble as an excuse, I pretended to lose balance and dumped her in her chair. She sat there, dizzy, fanning herself with a serviette. When she regained her breath, she looked at me solemnly and nodded her head, as if confirming the rightness of something she'd just been thinking. The plain truth is that the Marquis is looking superb tonight, she said. I, returning the compliment, replied: Not nearly as superb as the Baroness.

A delightful pantomime (Krugger decides), but I imagine that your mother, what with the champagne and all that bending and turning, must have been feeling a little sick.

Perhaps (I allow), but the fact is that two hours after supper she still showed not the slightest intention of ending the farce. I took the dirty dishes to the kitchen, leaving her, sunk in her chair with her eyes shut, and a surging violin. When I came back into the dining room, she asked me to sit beside her and she began to bewail how rapidly time passes. Then we got involved in a dialogue of the deaf. She spoke about loneliness and old age. While I talked about the pleasure of sharing in a common task and about the future. Your mother no longer has a future, she murmured brokenly, perhaps hoping I'd comfort her. I said that work, decent work, was not only a moral obligation for all men, but also the best possible diversion, the only one that could give life a bit of flavour. She finally realized that the whole pro-duction she'd mounted hadn't been a bit of use and, at once, she again decided on a change of tactics.

At that time of night? (Krugger is surprised).

A good question (I say), it would then be already one-thirty in the morning. But when she lets her hair down, my mother isn't put off by such details. So, when the champagne ran out, she made do with brandy and was silent for a moment or two. Then, out of the blue, she asked me where this Bank was. Cardinal Ceballos Square, I say, at least, that's the address the letter gave. Isn't that near Speaker Río Avenue? is her next question. Once again, it was as if butter wouldn't melt in her mouth. I said yes, it was close by, and then she wanted to know the route I was going to take to get here. I replied that I'd take the shortest, but she wanted me to give her more details.

I find that quite incredible (Krugger mutters). Did you give them?

I had no alternative (I answer), because if I hadn't, she would've made a fuss. Don't worry, I shan't get lost (I said). The interview's arranged for two p.m., but I'm planning to allow enough time to get there on foot. So I'll go down Conqueror Aguirre Avenue, turn into Henry the Sorrowful Boulevard and then along Astronaut Gonzalo Street. I'll cross St Arthur's Square and continue along Cabinboy Serras Street, Foresail Alley, Starboard Street and Windward Passage. From there, going down Louis the Accurate, Sublieutenant Herrero, Archpriest Clavero, Composer Alonso and Speaker Río, I'll reach Cardinal Ceballos Square. While I was reciting this run of street names, she listened suspiciously. She said she was surprised I knew the route so exactly, considering she couldn't remember our having been in that part of the city together. You must have escaped from home one night when I was asleep, she accused me, with a pointing finger. I swore I hadn't, that I'd never been in that area and that if I knew the names of the streets, it was because I'd learnt them by heart from a street plan I had in my room, on which I'd marked the route to follow.

I must note down that detail on your credit side (interrupted Krugger, somewhat smugly). We rate foresight very highly in this Bank.

5

I recognize I'm lucky to have someone to whom I can tell all my troubles. This long interview (whether it ends providing me with a job or not) at least allows me to ease my conscience. So I go on to tell Krugger that my mother continued to be suspicious and asked me to show her the street plan.

I went to fetch it (I report) and I spread it out on her lap. There you are, I said. But don't imagine she was satisfied. She moved the standard lamp next to her chair and started to study it like someone trying to decipher hieroglyphics. She finally decided she didn't like my route because the last section went through a dangerous area. She was referring to the Fishermen's Quarter, full of bars with a bad reputation and the lowest type of brothel, with whores who, according to her, come down into the street to pick up passers-by. Wasn't it in Cabinboy Serras Street (she queried) where they slit the throat of a city policeman a couple of weeks back?

It was a postman (Krugger amends, raising his right hand) who got his throat slit, not a city policeman.

He recalls that the postman in question, using the excuse of having a registered letter to deliver, slipped into a flat and went to bed with the lady of the house who, it seems, willingly received him. The husband returned home sooner than expected and surprised them *in flagrante delicto*. I'm told that similar situations arise in the best families and in the smartest quarters.

That's what I told my mother (I proceed, pleased that, for once, Krugger's point of view coincides with mine), but she, ignoring this, suggested another route which by-passed the Fishermen's Quarter and was, in her opinion, less dangerous than the one I'd chosen. She agreed I could go down Conqueror Aguirre, but then, she advised that, instead of turning into Henry the Sorrowful Boulevard, I took Marquis of Fairview, then turned into Deputy-Governor Losada and followed Menhir Promenade and the Ring Road, so ending up in Cardinal Ceballos Square. I began to lose patience and had to bite my lip to avoid flaring up. I said all right, all paths lead to Rome, but she disagreed, saying that was far from true and some paths led to damnation and hell. Can you imagine what it was like, listening to all that nonsense at two in the morning?

Apart from everything else (I go on to tell him), bear in mind that the route she was proposing meant a detour of one or two miles, which, if I'd taken any notice, would've meant my leaving home two or three hours earlier than I'd planned. You're right (my mother admitted, when I pointed this out), but that way you'll be better able to throw your pursuers off the scent. Her comment, which was made quite seriously (even in lowered voice, as if she were frightened of being overheard by somebody), was the last straw. Who's going to waste his time pursuing me? (I shouted). Who's going to worry about what I do or don't do? Why do you insist on imagining that I'm such an important person?

It's obvious (Krugger observes) that your lady mother is obsessed with the risk of losing you.

Look, I'll tell you openly (I stress), if I believed she was mad, I shouldn't be bothering you with all this, because nobody can be blamed for being mad. But, of course, my mother isn't mad. Her trouble (as you'll have already appreciated) is only a psychological deviation, the manias of a sick old wreck, the psychopathic fantasies of an ancient reactionary who stubbornly insists on believing nothing has changed in the last fifty years.

Do you really think something has changed? (Krugger inquires).

I think so (I reply, smiling). Fifty years ago, for example, I still hadn't been born. And banks didn't need night-watchmen. A simple porter sufficed.

Go on with your story (Krugger requests, accepting my irony). Go on talking about your poor mother's phantoms.

That's exactly what I told her (I continue), that she was seeing phantoms and imagining things. All right (I let out), you find the streets in the Fishermen's Quarter dangerous, but if we're talking about that, why aren't you also bothered about that eight-year-old girl who was raped in the gardens of the Public Library, right by the Ring Road, only a week ago?

Krugger remembers that crime, too. He specifies that on that occasion the attacker was an unemployed bricklayer who'd spent the morning in the library reading Aristotle's *Metaphysics*, a fact (made much of in the press) which forced him to think yet again about the dangers of unsuitable or excessive reading.

My mother (I continue, ignoring his observation), refusing to let me have the last word, tried to exonerate the bricklayer. She even dared to say that the raped girl was one of those perverse corrupters of older men, fond of starting fires which then couldn't be put out. What kind of fire could a little girl of eight start? I shouted indignantly. I was really seeing red again. Finally, I managed to control myself and, after taking a deep breath, I sighed and admitted that the route she was suggesting was a sensible one and that the worst of the streets she'd chosen was preferable to the best in the Fishermen's Quarter. I also recognized that the tenants of the Ring Road's big town houses had little in common with the people who were crowded together in the murky lodging houses of the Fishermen's Quarter. I duly allowed all this but then, with a condescending smile, I said that those differences didn't mean that the rich were, by definition, less dangerous than the poor through the mere fact of being rich. Once again, she picked up the gauntlet. She raised her hand as if she were going to take an oath and assured me that she had nothing against the poor. She even recognized that there were cases in which poverty became the best way to achieve inner perfection. She used the same words, more or less, as you did earlier when justifying the merits of the Bank's nightwatchmen. But then, with one of her sharp smiles, she added that, nevertheless, crime and sedition were more frequent among the poor than among the rich, and this was statistically demonstrable.

Once more, Krugger's in agreement with my mother. He declares it's a fairly common error to imagine that people who lack material wealth can only permit themselves the pleasure of self-denial. If nothing else (he points out), there remains the pleasure of revenge.

She also spoke of revenge (I carry on), and, among the nonsense, I remember that she pointed out that the inhabitants of the Fishermen's Quarter might set upon me for the simple reason that I lived in a sunny flat with ten rooms in the upper part of the city. How are they

going to know all that? I asked her. She said it would
be enough for them to see my face, that they could smell
it a mile off. Let's suppose for a moment you're right (I
then replied), if those people really want revenge, why
don't they look for someone who's really rich? Who am
I, after all? In which bank do I keep my millions?

In a way (Krugger allows, giving me another of his
long looks), your power of rejoinder I find admirable.
You, my friend, are a worthy son of your mother.

The easiest thing (I tell him) would have been to admit
her right and to ask leave to go off to bed, especially
bearing in mind what time it was. I said to myself, however,
that to leave her then could be taken as desertion, or as
a surrender because of exhaustion, and I decided to fight
on in the breach. I drew to her notice (because it's true)
the fact that we were almost as poor as the people in the
Fishermen's Quarter, that our flat had a low controlled
rent and that if we had to move house today, there'd be
nothing for it but to look for lodging in some half-built
suburb. As you can imagine, she received my remark like
a blow, especially because she knew that I had more
right on my side than a saint. She looked at me in silence,
and then admitted that I wasn't wrong in supposing we
weren't rich and that, compared with some, we could
even be considered poor. But then she distinguished
between the different types of poverty. There isn't a silly
bone in your body (she said) and you know very well
that fifteen or twenty years of economic austerity aren't
enough for one to take on the nature of the genuine poor.

I don't understand that, breathes Krugger.

I imagine (I explain to him) that what she meant to
say was that our poverty, however bad, would never be
like that other type of poverty which is inherited, generation after generation, and which ends up engendering
a special sort of sensibility in its most recent victims.

Krugger slowly nods his head. It surprises him not to have understood the thrust of my mother's words sooner; he considers her right in assuming that there are at least two types of poor. He also thinks that the poor of always, the historic poor (whose right to live he recognizes, in spite of everything), rejoice and suffer in a different way from us.

It seems to me (he considers) that these people are stirred by different stimuli. They're fellow-humans, but less so. Much less human than you and I, for example. And don't run away thinking that, by saying this, I'm a reactionary of the old school. Working in this Bank I've learnt to put people into two big groupings: those who have money and those who don't. I'm not worried about lineage or the number of quarterings on a shield, what I'm concerned with are our clients' current accounts and, ultimately, the education which only money can buy. All the rest's a load of rubbish. And in this matter things proceed as they always have, they haven't changed all that much in the last fifty years. The historic poor, even if they suddenly better their lot, need at least two or three generations before that can approach us in matters of sensibility.

His distant, arrogant smile forces me to look at the floor. It'll be better if I don't get too many false ideas about this interview's outcome.

And so (he ends up pronouncing) I don't know if the inhabitants of the Fishermen's Quarter, just by looking at your face, can guess that you live in a sunny flat in the upper part of the city. But I'm convinced – and thereby fully concur with your lady mother – that for such people you'll always be an effete young gentleman who now, in his recently acquired maturity, has the eccentric whim of starting work. Your mother's right, my friend: today's poor will not approve of such frivolity.

He lights another cigarette (he's already smoked half the packet during this interview) and waits for me to say something in my own defence. I can't think of anything: his arguments are as absurd as they are demoralizing. I cross my arms, change the position of my legs and watch the rain. It suddenly occurs to me that if it rains from above downwards, it's precisely so that we, who are below, get wet. If it rained the other way round (I reason, amused by my bright idea), they'd get wet, the ones who are on top. Krugger, meanwhile, removes the holder from his mouth and proceeds to raise another point which isn't quite clear.

A moment ago (he remarks) you said you kept a street guide in your room and that you'd marked the route here in red on the plan. I observed that you'd shown commendable foresight, but now I'm seeing things from another angle. I'm wondering if it should be taken as normal for a lad of your age, who has to journey no more than a few hundred yards in his own city, to learn the names of all the streets by heart. Don't you think that all your caution could mean you're frightened of facing the exterior world which your lady mother's so keen to protect you from?

He leans on the arm of the chair and smiles, pleased with his shrewdness.

I can just picture you (he says) in the privacy of your room tracing the best route to follow with a trembling hand. I see you as a general studying the advance of his troops across enemy territory. Of course, you didn't even do military service and can't have the slightest idea what a general must feel at such moments.

I think (I reply) I can deem myself my own soldier.

Yes, yes (retorts Krugger), your own soldier, the only soldier in your own army. But, as I see it, an excessively prudent soldier, when, sometimes at least, real prudence consists in being bold.

But (I ask, increasingly angry) don't you think that my lady mother – as you call her – also overdoes it?

No, he doesn't think so. He presumes to be very clear about this. He says that no mother can be excessively prudent when it's a question of safeguarding her children's happiness. What happens, in his opinion, is that they act under the dictates of mysterious premonitions, which not even they are capable of explaining. Therefore, he very well understands my mother's anxiety while trying, uselessly, to make me perceive something she saw so clearly.

What would you do (he asks me) if you saw a blind man about to fall into an abyss?

I find it an insulting comparison and I tell him that if he really believes that I can be equated with a blind man, it's better if we terminate the interview. It doesn't seem to me fair (I protest) to call a man blind whose only dream is to shape his own fate.

He forces a smile and stretches his arms towards me, warding off my reproaches. He understands my being cross and wants to make it quite clear that nothing he says or thinks can be sufficient reason for interrupting the interview before the time allowed for it has run out. He indicates that I still have half an hour to convince him I'm the ideal candidate.

It may be (he says) you'll finally manage to make a case for yourself.

Do you think (I ask him) it's worth while embarking on further confidences?

Come now, keep on to the end (he urges). I want to know how the night finished up, what time you got to bed and if you finally came to some agreement about the route.

Maybe, instead of going on with that subject, I should

speak to him about the hours and hours over these last years that I've spent leaning out of the window of my room, gazing at the city's towers in the distance. Perhaps I should talk to him about my lonely nights by that same window-ledge, bewitched by the constellation of distant, lit up windows, while my mother, shouting from her armchair, said it was time for me to be in bed.

Did you come to some agreement? (he insists).

I'm about to say no, that we didn't come to any agreement, but there's a knock on the door. The messenger, as silently as a sacristan, comes into the office and gives back to Krugger the same envelope he'd taken away earlier. The photo of the girl with the defiant attitude is still there. Krugger reads the attached short message, written in the Director's own handwriting. He sighs and sits sunk in deep thought. It's easy to guess that the Director has flatly rejected his candidate, and that he's taking this rejection as a personal failure, with unforeseeable consequences.

Here we have (he says to me) the trials and tribulations of an employee who thought himself little short of infallible.

I can feel in my own throat the knot that's forming in his. He manages an ashen smile and confirms that, as I'd supposed, the Director General has rejected the dark girl. He's trying to appear calm, but the pupils of his eyes are flickering like two small flames in a rarefied atmosphere.

The trouble is (I say) that neither you nor I know a lot about women.

He doesn't reply, limiting himself to a confused smile. He tears the photo into four pieces, which he lets fall into the wastepaper basket. He puts the handwritten note between two pages of his desk-top diary, extracts from the drawer the photographs he'd earlier discarded and examines them one by one. He's bewildered and ends up shrugging his shoulders. He shows me a blonde's portrait in which the only attraction he can find is that of youth, and wants to have my opinion. I decline with a vigorous nod and tell him it seems strange to me that after working so long in the Bank he hasn't his bosses' tastes at his fingertips. I've realized that, at this moment, I'm the stronger of the two and I want to humiliate him for his contemptuous attitude a few minutes ago.

Men's tastes (he whispers, without looking up from the photos) change over the years.

He tries hard to keep a smile on his lips, but he doesn't manage to mask his concern, and the tension of his facial muscles makes him look younger. Finally, he pushes a new candidate's photo in the envelope and arches his eyebrows, as if he didn't feel very sure of his choice. I'm sceptical and say that most likely he's making another mistake.

You and I only understand mothers (I tell him).

I try to catch his eye, but can't. He clicks his tongue, pulls the photo from the envelope and starts comparing them again. At the same time, he claims that he's a man of quick decisions, that he doesn't like to keep people waiting and that therefore he makes mistakes. Then he shakes his head and puts the photos back in the folder. It's a way of recognizing that he's presently not in a fit state to choose the ideal candidate. He lifts a fresh cigarette to his lips and lights it with a shaking hand. It's the first time I see him inhale the smoke convincingly, since the interview began.

This time (he says, following up his train of thought), I can't allow myself the luxury of being wrong. I'll take the photos home and spend the weekend studying them. I'll do it calmly, because pressure is the father of failure.

He puts the folder in the drawer and rubs his hands,

trying to instil confidence in himself. When I observe that, because of this business with the photos, he won't be able to read his poems this weekend, he puts his finger on his lips, commanding silence.

We'll shelve that (he whispers) and, till Monday, we'll also shelve the photographs.

I reply telling him that the latter will only be shelved when the Director General approves a new candidate and that's not going to be easy (I add) because women aren't exactly your strong point.

You and I (I repeat, pressing my advantage) don't know much about women.

Who can possibly presume to understand them? (he asks me, sighing).

I propose that we dedicate the interview's remaining time to talking about women, other than our mothers, of course; about those other women, of whom we, he as much as I, have fruitlessly dreamt. For a moment his gaze brightens. He stubs out his cigarette in the ashtray, glances at his wristwatch and says that we still have half an hour's conversation. Too much time, in his opinion, to lose talking about women. He requests me to go on with my account up to when I came into this office full of hope, thinking, perhaps, that everything was going to be much simpler.

6

The office (which has been growing noticeably darker over the last few minutes) is lit up by a stroke of lightning. Krugger, perhaps surprised by the flash, sits up even straighter in his chair and waits for the thunder-clap with a defiant expression. He's recovered his self-confidence and once again takes command of the situation. He insists on my continuing my story to its end and advises me not to waste the opportunity I'm being offered, because I need to confess to somebody and he's the only person who'll listen to me, albeit for professional reasons.

I must admit he's right. I'd not find anyone else who'd want to hear me out. They'd be bored stiff and tell me to go to hell at the very start.

No, we didn't agree about the route (I say, responding to his last question), but I went on trying to make her understand that the difference between the inhabitants of the Fishermen's Quarter and the people who live in the better parts of the city was not as great as she thought. One of my arguments was to tell her that, after all, everybody is born naked and dies alone. That was the end of it. When she heard me talk about death, she jumped up from her chair, shut herself in her room and started to sob bitterly.

Krugger asks me if my mother is frightened by the idea
of dying, and I tell him yes, that she can't stand people
talking about death (not even that of others) and that, a
couple of years ago, she didn't want to be told about the
death of a sister who, to cap it all, was her only surviving
one.

Sometimes (I proceed) I think that she treats me as if
I were a child because that way she feels younger and
further off from the end.

Did you go to comfort her? Krugger inquires.

I didn't (I reply) because I thought it was better to
leave her in peace to see if she'd fall asleep. I also needed
to be alone, so I stayed in my chair, thinking about
today's appointment with you and trying to sort things
out in my mind. As you can imagine, after spending the
whole day arguing, my nerves were as taut as guitar
strings. To calm myself down – and to restore my spirits
– I did what I'd done on so many other occasions: I went
to my room, opened the window wide and confronted
the night. Don't laugh, but in a certain way that's like
confronting life. I put out the light so that nobody could
see me and began to count those windows which, at that
late hour (it would've already gone three), were still lit
up. So you see: some count sheep to get to sleep; I count
windows. After a while I tiptoed out into the passage,
approached my mother's bedroom, stuck my ear to the
door and heard her snoring peacefully. I didn't want to
consider that she was still awake, pretending she was
asleep, but in fact pondering fresh objections.

There's another thunder-clap (a crisp, forthright
report, which shakes the window-panes), and Krugger
again glances fleetingly at the window.

Then I went back to my room (I continue), and got into
bed. But don't go thinking it was easy for me to get to

sleep. I felt as nervous as a jelly, thinking that it was the first time (forgive me if I exaggerate a little) I was – at my own risk – going to confront a world which, up till then, I'd always seen from the grandstand. I spent a long time with my eyes shut, seeing if I could get to sleep, but it was useless. Then I sat on the bed and, by torchlight (I didn't turn on the light so that my mother, if she woke up, wouldn't come in and be a nuisance), I pored over the street plan. You must think I was acting like a general preparing for battle, and you are right, because it was the first big battle of my life. What's true is that I was feeling more and more anxious about the possibility that, in spite of all my efforts, I could end up losing my way. I think that would've been like killing myself. Anyway, just as dawn was breaking, I managed to doze off, and this morning I woke up a little before eight, in other words I slept only two or three hours. An hour later, at nine, I went into the dining-room and there she was, waiting for me with breakfast ready. I said good morning as if there was such a thing and she answered with a smile. She was looking well, fresh as a daisy, in her blue flannel dressing-gown and a scrubbed face without any make-up. The dining room was back to normal, no candlesticks and that sort of nonsense. She'd cleaned it from top to bottom and was sitting in her usual place, with a steaming coffee-pot and hot toast. The great day's arrived, she announced, while she filled my coffee cup with a hand that didn't tremble.

An unconditional surrender (Krugger supposes).

None of your unconditional surrenders (I correct him), on the contrary. I immediately understood that she was clearing the ground and gathering together all her remaining strength to launch a final offensive. She lifted her cup to her mouth and, over it, gave me a searching look. Very well, my little Juanito (she said, as if accepting the inevitable), you've chosen your own destiny, but no one can blame me for not having acted like a good mother.

I find it delightful that she still calls you little Juanito at your age, murmurs Krugger, looking at me tenderly.

A fresh peal of thunder shakes the window-panes again, and the rain gets heavier. The storm must now be right overhead.

She pours me another cup of coffee (I continue) and, while doing so, asks me what I've decided to wear for this appointment. My blue jacket and grey trousers, I told her, in other words, what I'm wearing now. She wrinkles her nose and reminds me that this jacket (the one you see) has frayed cuffs, and that the trousers are beginning to go at the knees. She advised me to attend this interview as well dressed as possible, as if I were going to a wedding. She also said that if you saw me in this jacket and these trousers you were going to think I was some unfortunate, because it's the habit that makes the monk. I recognized she wasn't entirely wrong and suggested wearing a check suit, which I've had for some time but worn little, so it still looks all right. It didn't seem good enough to her and she justified her disapproval with some argument or other. She said that one recognized the bird by its feathers and the man by his clothes and that, given my interest in working in this Bank, I couldn't take the risk that you, seeing me badly dressed, might think that I had to work through necessity. In which case you'd surely get rid of me on some pretext or other, she pronounced.

Not a bit of it (says Krugger). On this occasion, your lady mother errs.

All I'm doing (I underline) is to repeat what she said. I don't pretend to analyse her thinking. I'm recounting everything, step by step and point by point, as you asked me to do at the outset. But I can say that my mother wasn't talking for the sake of it and that everything had been carefully programmed, perhaps this very morning before I got up, or maybe last night, while she was pretending to snore and poor me thought she was sleeping. So, at the right moment, she brought her little girl's voice into play and suggested that I should wear my father's suit, like last night. I flatly refused, claiming it was too tight and barely let me move my arms. Then she took me to her bedroom, opened her wardrobe doors wide and said there I could find half a dozen suits my father had left almost unworn. I could wear the one I liked most. She left me on my own so I could choose in peace, but I didn't know where to begin. Apart from the suits, I counted six or seven odd jackets and a similar number of pairs of trousers. My mother keeps all his clothing in plastic covers, as if she's still expecting my father to return home without any warning.

We're almost in the dark and Krugger decides to turn on the light he has on his desk. He thus has at his disposal a new device for demarcation and he positions the shade so that the light shines directly on my face. He asks me how long it's been since my father died, twenty-five years I tell him, and he throws me an amused glance.

I imagine (he says) your father's clothes are somewhat out of fashion.

I overlooked that detail this morning (I reply). All I know is that, when my mother spoke about the need to appear at the interview well dressed, I began to worry about what the Bank's preference would be, regarding clothing. I told myself you might be austere people, partial to sobriety and dark colours, on the other hand, you could be jolly folk, fond of gay colours and a certain dash. There was a moment when I considered trying on all the suits and getting her to tell me which one suited me most. But the hands of the clock were going round, the hour of the interview was getting closer and I could no longer waste time on such experiments. I asked her to choose the one she thought most suitable. We returned to her bedroom, she put her arm into the wardrobe and brought out, in quick succession, a blue double-breasted jacket with gold buttons, a salmon pink shirt and green corduroy trousers. Instead of an ordinary tie (which doesn't afford much scope for being different), she chose a red-spotted bow tie.

Quite a daring outfit, Krugger allows, without losing his slight smile.

She justified her choice with a variety of arguments (I continue). She told me that fortune smiles on the brave, that this country's people were over-fond of dark colours and that men especially suffered from excessive severity of dress, as if, when choosing our wardrobe, we are seized by the fear of ridicule.

Absolutely (interrupts Krugger, who once more praises my mother's powers of discernment). I agree that the people of this country are too fond of dark colours, especially black.

Black (I maintain) is the colour which perhaps best corresponds with our collective frustration. My mother was taking this strange national characteristic into account. Imagine (she said) turning up at that Bank (almost certainly run by foreigners) in an old blue jacket which looks black in electric light and which, what's more, has frayed cuffs. What are those people going to think? Without fail, they're going to think you're some poor frustrated wretch, some unfortunate who's full of resentment, who's always boasted of despising life's pleasant, simple things, but who when least expected gets his own back, reaching for the fruit hitherto always forbidden him...Wear what I say. Stop debating and take heed. Then they'll say here we have a bold young lad, a big-hearted happy youth, with no traumas. A repentent *chansonnier* who has drained pleasure's cup to its bottom and now, today, tired of so many nights of wine and roses, has come to his senses and genuinely wants to start work. She only half-convinced me, but I screwed up my courage and dressed as she suggested: a blue jacket with gold buttons, green corduroy trousers and a red-spotted bow tie. I wasn't very sure, but as soon as I saw myself full length in the wardrobe mirror, I could only bellow with laughter: I understood everything. The trousers only reached to my ankles and the jacket would've been tight on a twelve-year-old boy. I went to the dining-room (she, as usual, was sitting in her armchair, waiting) and I asked her how I looked. Like a prince, she whispered, looking at me proudly.

Perhaps that's how she saw you (Krugger suggests), perhaps she really saw you changed into a prince.

Don't be as ingenuous as I was (I tell him), because what my mother was trying to achieve was for me to present myself in this Bank dressed like a clown or an irresponsible dandy, so that you'd send me packing as soon as I entered the doorway and before I'd time to give my name. Do you see the point now? I let fly without holding anything back. I told her I'd discovered her game, that she hadn't taken me in, and she, finally, dropped her mask. Once again, she showed her teeth. Her solicitous expression vanished and she admitted that, yes, all she was seeking was that you would rule out my candidature as soon as you saw me. She brandished her old argument and said that only in this way could she save me from the humiliation of working for a foreign bank. It's that business of humiliation again, is it? (I exclaimed). Are you again going to tell me they still haven't forgiven us the burning of heretics? She, after a moment's thought, finally resorted to her last and definitive argument, which she hadn't yet dared to use. She gave me a pathetic look and asked: Do these people know you've got six fingers on each hand? Did you tell them that in your letter?

Krugger gasps with surprise and the cigarette holder falls from his mouth. He can't believe what he's heard and he asks me to show him my hands.

There you are, nothing from another world (I say, showing him them), a simple anatomical rarity. Six fingers on the left hand and six on the right. A total of twelve.

He seems fascinated by my hands, can't take his eyes off them. Then he realizes that his bewilderment isn't what best suits a man of the world and he shakes his head.

Anyway (he says, with deliberate urbanity), it would've been worse to have been born with two heads.

That is something you should say to my mother (I explain), because she's always thought that having six fingers on each hand is a defect which disqualifies me for ever. When we go out together she makes me walk with my hands in my pockets. I told her I hadn't recorded this detail in my letter and she thought I'd not done so on purpose so that you would believe the sender was a normal person. Now we'll see what sort of face they'll make when they see you, she muttered. I replied saying I considered myself to be a normal man and she laughed aloud and called me a monster. Which was as if she'd insulted herself. Then I went back to my room, took off the fancy costume I had on and dressed in what I'm wearing now.

Krugger's looking at his long, tapering hands.

When I'd recovered my normal aspect (I go on to tell him) I also recovered a part of the calm and confidence I'd lost. I returned to the dining-room and was ready to give her the *coup de grâce*. All right (I said), assuming that I am in fact a monster, to stop being one all I have to do is put my hands in my pockets. See how easy it is to arrange things. She took what I said at face value and said that no one could work with his hands in his pockets. Her lack of a sense of humour unhinged me. All right (I said), I'm a monster. But that doesn't frighten anybody any more, because the world today is full of all kinds of monsters. In fact, they are the ones who've got on best. The press, radio and television are on their side. They are even protected by Social Security. Who then is going to care that I've got six fingers on each hand?

It's continuing to rain violently and for a moment I fear that it may continue the deluge until the day of the Last Judgement. Krugger clears his throat forcefully, coughing up from his lungs, and he takes out his handkerchief. Then he lifts his head and excuses himself with a look.

All these final posturings (I continue) happened between eleven and half past, but we still went on talking for quite a bit longer. She was sitting in her armchair, like a queen on the point of seeing herself dethroned, but without losing her nerve. She recapitulated all the nonsense she'd been spouting up till then and, smiling, I listened without interrupting her. She repeated that I had no need to work, that it wasn't fair to leave her on her own all day, that I was going to be terribly humiliated, and that I'd be despatching her to the cemetery in next to no time. She also repeated that, whether I liked it or not, I couldn't consider myself normal: I was a freak of nature and she was the only person in the world who could tell me so. At that point, still smiling, I asked her if she considered herself normal. She said no, she wasn't normal either, but precisely for that reason, because we were twin souls, we were condemned to understand and protect each other throughout life. Her voice broke, she leant her head against the back of the chair and managed to shed a few tears. I think I've said everything now, she whispered, as if taking leave of life. But a moment later, she told me I could do what I like and go to the devil, but I should face the possibility of not finding her at home when I got back from this interview.

Did you face up to that risk? (Krugger inquires). Did you come here deliberately running the risk of not seeing her again? He can't understand the coldness and egotism of children. He recalls the tortoise-man he interviewed a couple of weeks ago, who was making fun of his mother while she was praying, at the entrance to the Bank, for her son's successful integration in the world of work and reputation.

Who is the guilty party? he whispers, arching his eyebrows.

He's sitting there with his head bowed, as if for lack of a convincing answer he wants to listen the better to the purring of his lungs. Then he raises his head and I read in his look the holy indignation of those who are impotently taking part in the ending of the only form of culture they can understand. Then he sighs and, finally, comes down on my mother's side. He adds that in the war between parents and children, he always sides with the former. He also confesses that he belongs to that group of men who advocate traditional values (now lost) and who do not hesitate to contribute their little grain of sand to the task of rebuilding the ancient structures of society.

He smiles sadly and blames himself for not having laid his cards on the table straight off.

Think what you like (he remarks), but if I were in your place, I'd leave this office immediately and run home to kneel at your mother's feet.

Don't worry so much about her (I reassure him). When I get home, no matter what the hour, I'll find her waiting for me with the table laid.

What if you're wrong on this occasion? (he retorts). What if, this time, you enter an irremediably empty house? What if you find your mother lying on the kitchen floor, with the gas turned on?

He seems on the point of tears. He gives me a brimming look and, encountering my puzzled expression, tries to hide his distress. He buries his face in a large orange handkerchief and blows his nose noisily.

Nevertheless, can we conclude (he asks). Tell me what your mother did this morning as you were leaving.

I wanted to kiss her brow (I recall), but she warded me off. Out in the street, I looked up at the balcony and could glimpse her behind the Venetian blind. I waved and she, realizing I'd seen her (or, who knows, noticing my right hand with its six fingers), she rushed out on to the balcony and began to shout madly that I should come back, that she'd forgive everything. I thought the best thing was to get out of her sight as quickly as possible, and I ran till I'd turned the first corner.

Krugger half-closes his eyes and leans his head on his right hand. He's silent for a couple of minutes, then, emerging from his thoughts, he sighs deeply.

Let's forget that unhappy lady now (he begs me), and tell me what you did when you found yourself alone in the city. The first part of your big dream was over. What did you do when you'd turned the first corner? Did you go on running? Did you stick to the envisaged route?

Yes (I said), I followed the streets I'd marked on the street-plan, but as I'd time to spare, when I reached St Arthur's Square, I bought a packet of seeds, sat on a bench and spent a while feeding the pigeons. Then I began to see things in a different light. I saw, for example, that not even pigeons could consider themselves free, in spite of having wings, because to survive they depend on what they can peck on the ground. I won't be free, simply by going to work, I said to myself. I saw that I was about to look out on a landscape that would end up boring me as much as the one I knew already. I'm telling you all this now because I know I haven't the slightest chance of being accepted. I'll end up telling you everything. When I was tired of sitting, I clapped my hands and the pigeons took off in flight. I left the square, went down Cabinboy Serras Street and, on reaching the junction with Foresail Alley, I ran into a demonstration with a display of red flags. I thought it was silly of them to choose such a narrow street. I took refuge in a doorway, let the demonstrators pass and went along Archpriest Clavero and Composer Alonso. When I reached Speaker Río Avenue, I came across another demonstration, almost certainly returning from Cardinal Ceballos Square. This time the flags were blue, but the shouting sounded as equally stubborn and boastful, although the tune was different. Which group should I join? I thought.

Krugger wants to know if I belong to some political grouping or, at least, sympathize with a particular party.

What does it matter (I ask him) when you're born with six fingers on each hand? Anyway (I can now say so clearly), it wasn't the city I was expecting to find. I've got the impression that people are walking about, sniffing the scent of a fire that's still distant, but inexorably approaching. But despite everything, I followed my route, striding purposefully and trying to convince myself that I too had my own banner. I'm a solitary soldier (I said to myself) who must advance towards his own destiny, a romantic, abandoned sharpshooter who will end up becoming his own general. But, as I told you a moment ago, I was no longer very sure it was worth while coming to see you. It was as if all my mother's suggestions and warnings of the last few days began to act together at the same time, having a cumulative effect. I also felt worried about the way you were going to direct this interview. I'll explain myself better: It's not that I was worried about being subjected to a general culture test (you soon found out I was a fairly well-read man); I worried about the likelihood of your asking me (instead of, what is the world's largest river, for example, or the capital of Denmark, or America's highest mountain) questions such as: Have you ever fired a pistol? Did you hit the target? What kind of target was it? A human being? A man? Did you leave him badly wounded, perhaps? In this last case, did you have sufficient guts to finish him off?

Krugger, smiling, nods. He admits they would not have been bad questions. He wants to know if, at the same time, I'd also felt worried about my six fingers.

Not about my fingers as such (I reply), but about the possibility that you might want to check whether this deformity could have generated some hidden inferiority complex capable, in its turn, of engendering an invincible hatred towards normally built people. I said to myself that if this happened I'd have to face another type of question. For example: Would you be likely to shoot someone you came across in the Bank's corridors (without positive proof that he's a thief), simply because you thought he didn't have conspicuous physical defects?

That isn't a bad question either (Krugger decides), and I'm immediately going to put it to you officially: Would you be capable of firing at a normally endowed person (perhaps a colleague) without valid or sufficient reason, in a sudden worsening of your inferiority complex?

I don't answer and he shrugs his shoulders, letting me know that what I can do with a pistol no longer matters. But he seizes the opportunity to go on about my hands. He says that if those additional digits had been on my feet, it wouldn't have mattered at all.

In order to maximize profits and to afford our share-holders good dividends (he explains), this Bank has always dispensed with concerns of an aesthetic nature. However, you've got too many fingers on your hands and that factor would've complicated your application, if it were not already fatally compromised by other circumstances. You can surely understand? That extra finger on your right hand must've suggested to you some additional problem at the moment of squeezing the trigger of your pistol. This Bank, my friend, when choosing its future employees, is guided solely by matters of efficiency. Do you follow me? Imagine one night on one of your rounds coming face to face with a thief. You unholster your pistol and get ready to fire: where are you going to put that supernumerary finger so that, at the vital moment, it doesn't obstruct your index finger's operation?

He pauses and moves his cigarette-holder from one side of his mouth to the other with the tip of his tongue.

How could you tell me earlier that you liked poetry? I ask him, with a smile.

My comment makes him frown. He replies saying that man's only poetry is the mother and that it's now high time this great truth was understood. Without losing my smile, I tell him I don't give a fig for my mother and I see him pale. He lets a couple of minutes elapse but the blood doesn't come back to his cheeks. Finally, he says that he prefers to believe that I'm mad and he wonders if it's necessary for children to lose their parents in order to learn to love them.

Do you want me to tell you now (he demands, in a broken voice), what my life has been since I lost my mother? Do you want me to speak about my sleepless nights, thinking about those blasted chick-peas?

Suddenly, I see everything clearly. And I tell him plainly, looking him straight in the eye and without giving my discovery more importance than might be given to the finding of an old summons among our papers.

It was you who killed your mother (I say), it was you who put the chick-peas on the staircase.

He gives me an astonished look, blinking furiously, and sits there with his mouth open. His right hand opens and closes spasmodically.

How it could have occurred to you (I insist) only God knows. You put some chick-peas on each step, hid yourself in the stairwell, and waited to see who would be the first victim. Perhaps you expected it would be one of the servants, but it was your mother.

He sits without reacting and without taking his gaze off me. His eyes are two little bits of ice. He goes on breathing with his mouth open and the wheezing of his lungs is increasingly acute. The noise of the rain, which continues to fall at a slant striking the window-panes, is a counterpoint to a very edgy silence.

It was you, I breathe, pointing my forefinger.

I immediately withdraw it but we continue looking each other in the eye, like two accomplices confronted by the body of a joint crime. Suddenly a clamour of angry voices, supported by a chorus of car horns, rises from the

street. Who are they? The demonstrators with red flags?
Those with blue? Another group of the disgruntled who,
at the last minute, decided to add itself to the general
outcry? Krugger, at last, begins to react. He gets up and
goes over to the window.

Anyway (he says, his back to me), since then, many
years have gone by.   .

Down below, the demonstrators' cries grow fainter and
then cease. Perhaps the rain has chilled their spirits. It
won't be long before I, too, have to face the downpour.
And what if, as Krugger suggested, my mother's decided
to leave me for ever?

Krugger returns to his seat behind the desk. The colour's come back to his cheeks. He locks the desk drawers
(it's a way of letting me know it's all over), and recognizes
that this interview (disregarding its outcome) has at least
occasioned our reciprocal confessions.

The best thing you can do now (he advises me) is to
go home and sit in your chair, facing your mother. You
haven't grievous sins to expiate.

What you're proposing (I say, overlooking the business of the chick-peas) is for me to desert.

To desert? (he exclaims). From what? Your obligation
to a society which mocks all your efforts to redeem it?
It's not worth while worrying about that, my friend. Save
yourself the trouble and avoid a lot of unpleasantness.
Who do you think you are? Have you ever seen yourself
in the mirror? Do you think you're as strong, intelligent
and handsome as your mother has led you to believe?

Perhaps you're right (I admit), maybe it's not worth
trying.

So the matter is closed (says Krugger, raising his voice
and placing the palms of his hands on the top of the
desk, as if to help him rise): I can now officially tell you

that your application for the post of nightwatchman in this Bank has been rejected. You have some virtues, but your defects (defects from the point of view of this Bank at least) are greater: you are too well-read, you like music, you've never used a firearm and, to top it all, you've got six fingers on each hand. Where do you think you can go with such a burden? Your mother knows only too well: men such as you must renounce the world, before the world rejects them.

Very well then (I murmur).

Moreover (he concludes), it's that very loving mother whom this Bank, which I represent, has the obligation to protect. Children are like lamps in a dark place, and we could never have allowed ourselves to leave your mother in darkness.

He opens the drawer of his desk again and hands me the little book of recipes. He wants me to give it to my mother, with his respects and admiration. He stands up, suppresses a yawn and places his hands behind his back. I stand up as well and try to smile. After being so long in the same position, my left leg has gone to sleep. There are people who begin to die from the feet up, it occurs to me.